THE LOST
OUTPOST

JOSHUA QUENTIN HAWK

ISBN: 978-1-63950-277-6 (sc)
ISBN: 978-1-63950-280-6 (e)

Gateway Towards Success

8063 MADISON AVE #1252
Indianapolis, IN 46227
+13176596889
www.writersapex.com

Other Books by Joshua Quention Hawk:

The Pearl Drop Killer

CONTENTS

CHAPTER ONE

GAMMA II RESEARCH STATION

"FIRE, COMMANDER!"

"Admiral Martinez?"

"I order you to fire and destroy that ship, now!"

He could not believe his ears. The Admiral wanted him to destroy the Alien ship rising from the planet, when in the past the Admiral had always wanted any new technology for himself, and he could never bring himself to kill, without just cause, and not even then, especially a new life-form, new technology. And as a scientist, he knew this was something worth studying, something new to learn. He could not bring himself to destroy it.

"I said fire, Commander! Or I will order your destruction!"

The Admiral had given him no choice. He could see the massive Alien ship now coming into view, and it was huge, spanning over a hundred kilometers in height and width, motionless and just hovering there above him in space. He tapped a few buttons on a panel to his right. Slowly his small fighter maneuvered up and above the massive Alien ship to gain a better angle of sight. From this better angle, above the massive Alien ship, he could see it completely, with all its battle damage and scarring, realizing the Alien ship was Ancient. His sensor panel lit up like a Christmas tree. An alarm sounded, then every panel in his fighter started flashing, and then a bright light illuminated and enveloped him, and then his ship, blinding his field of vision.

He had no memory of who he was, where he was going, or where he had been—just a pounding need to keep walking. The pounding need was from his throbbing headache, a deep gash along his left leg, and a cut over his right eye. Pausing a moment, catching his breath, realizing he was not limping but dragging his leg, his vision was blurred, and it was pitch-black. He could not see anything, except a single red flashing light off somewhere in the distance.

From the darkness, he could tell it was night. He could not tell where he was. There was no moon, and he could not recognize the stars. Through his foggy memory, he was in an open, and barren place. *A desert,* he thought.

Feeling more blood running down his leg and the pain becoming more intense, he tightened his makeshift tourniquet, which rested above his left knee, but he had no memory of putting it there. He pulled the tourniquet tighter, feeling the blood slow and the pain easing. He rubbed his face, feeling a week's growth of facial hair, and then ran his fingers through his black hair, feeling the cut over his right eye. He just wanted to lie down and sleep, but he knew if he did, he would never get up again. He pushed on slowly toward the red light, which he knew was still far off in the distance, and then he heard a loud noise coming from ahead of him, then over the top of him, getting louder as it got closer. The sand started to kick up. *A spacecraft of some kind,* he thought.

The spacecraft positioned itself overhead as a bright light washed over him, nearly blinding him. He waved up at the spacecraft, hoping whoever it was would help him. The light was too bright. He covered his eyes. He yelled, but could only manage a cough, "Help me!"

The bright light enveloped him, and it started changing colors, blue, orange, and finally green. Then as suddenly as it started, it was gone, and silent again. He began to wonder if he had seen and heard it, or was it just his confused mind playing tricks?

He braced himself once more and looked around, found his old friend, the single red light, and continued on his trek.

He slipped, slid, and fell face-first into something wet, a cold wet substance, and jumped back, waking him from his fog. The cold water ran through the cut along his forehead, which began to pulse harder, the pain became too much to bear, and he passed out.

Shivering from the cold night air, the bright orange morning rays shined through his eyelids, waking him, and intensifying his headache once again. He covered his eyes and tried to focus on his new surroundings. With only a few hours of sleep, and to his amazement, he could now see where the red light was coming from; it was a beacon light, set atop an oversized dome. The structure was huge, but he could only see two elongated legs protruding from the central hub, which he somehow maneuvered through the night before with his scrambled mind.

In a flash, it came to him, a habitat ring, a completely contained environmental structure. He had been in structures like this before, but this one was not familiar. He did not recognize it or was his mind still playing tricks, like the spacecraft. The habitat ring enclosed a completely livable structure, with many rooms to accommodate the crews, five to six legs protruding out in varying lengths, two legs shorter than the rest for landing pads, on opposite ends.

The air was cool, still, and quiet. *Too quiet,* he thought as he continued to study his new surroundings and noticed the substance he had fallen into the night before, was a manmade lake, adjacent to the dome.

Its function was to take moisture from the air, condense it, and store it for the station's use. He slowly maneuvered around the lake to the far side, near the pumping station, seeing five oversized polyvinyl chloride pipes entering the lake from the structure, with three small boxes about two hundred by two hundred centimeters squared on top as moister intake filters.

He lay down, moved the water around, and took a sip. It was cool and tasted good. He drank his fill, fast, and washed his face, hands, and wounds the best he could. He retightened his makeshift tourniquet and stood again, a bit wobbly, he felt the numbness leaving his leg and the pain returning. He limped along the structure, to an adjacent room, protruding from the dome, with a large window. He looked inside, but it was dirty and dusty.

He took the cuff of his brown tattered and torn flight suit and rubbed the dirt away gaining a better view.

Looking inside, he saw three environmental suits, blue, black, and white, hanging on the wall, with black visors across the helmets, they looked as if tight to the body when worn. The white suit was turned some, facing him, and he could make out a box on its back with controls, a small oxygen cylinder, and boots resting on the deck, a door near the far end to his right, and another door around the corner to his left, which he could barely make out.

He hobbled around the corner and looked over the doorframe. He sees a panel down along his right side, with a keypad, and three small bulbs resting above—a black number pad with neon yellow numbers. The center bulb started to flash green, and with instinct, he tapped it. The door popped open a few centimeters, and he pushed it the rest of the way.

He felt the warm air exiting the room, and it was like a warm summer breeze back home in Texas, along the Gulf of Mexico. He stepped in dragging his wounded leg over the slightly raised threshold.

The only light in the room was coming from the dust and dirt-covered window which he looked through moments before. Searching the room, he opened two of the three lockers on the sidewall to his right and looked through the shelf unit nearest the environmental suits and found a set of shelves on the opposite wall, above and below the large window. It was a prep room for different environments, for off-world teams, hostile environments, and non-oxygen environments, like a moon or dead planet, which this world was neither.

He searched more. In the last locker, he found a few flashlights, oxygen tanks, and a small silver toolbox, with a couple of canteens, then closed the locker and walked around the corner to the other door he had partially seen from the outside. There was an identical panel in the doorframe.

He stepped. The green bulb flashed, sensing him, and he pushed it. The door popped open, and he pushed it the rest of the way. *I must not be a threat,* he thought.

Leaning against the doorframe, catching his breath, and feeling the pain in his leg throbbing harder, he poked his head in and looked around, first to the right, and then to the left. Bracing himself against the doorframe, he stepped into the corridor with his good leg first and then his other. He was now inside the structure and in a long corridor. He could feel the cool air from the environmental system, compared to heat from outside. To his left was an adjacent corridor two meters down. At the end of the hall behind him, he could see another corridor slightly to the right.

He ran his hands over the white walls on either side of him, feeling the metallic plastic surface, and having no indentions or grooves. He looked down at the carpet, which was dark brown with beige lines running along each side near the walls. He had another sense of déjà vu but continued.

He continued down the long corridor and turned right down into another corridor. As he turned down this corner, he saw another door, he stepped up, and this time it opened a few centimeters for him. He pushed it the rest of the way and laughed.

On his first try, he found the medical bay. The medical bay was large, one of the larger rooms, and back along the far wall from the door sat three medical beds protruding from the wall, each with black pads, and small black blankets folded near the foot, large circular light fixtures with four separate lights, each unit hanging above each bed. A long countertop ran along the wall toward the back, a black marble countertop and white drawers, and a large wall mirror, only running half the length of the room. Across the room connected to the wall was a large shelf, a console, a chair with a high back, and a metal chair with black padding. A large metallic door, down past the mirror, COLD STORAGE in red on its front.

On the wall to his right, two smaller panels embedded, one with a group of buttons, multiple colors, the next one up having a small vid screen and three buttons, colored black, green, and white, and each labeled SYS, ENV, and COM.

He pressed the COM button, "Hello, anyone here?" Shouting over the COM, but only hearing his weakened voice echoing through the structure, he walked around the room slowly, looking through each drawer. In the first few, he only finds linens and scrubs, but in the fourth drawer, he finds to his amazement a medical kit. A small silver case with a large red cross on its lid, and found a hypodermic unit, a small pistol-like device with a small needle attached along the barrel, and a few smaller cylinders, under it, each labeled Hydro-cord. Hydro-codeine, for pain, he quickly jabbed one tube into the handle, hearing a hissing sound as they connected, jabbing the needle into his good leg, and pulled the trigger, and heard another hissing sound, and the pain was gone, but he knew it would not last. He took a second tube out of the case and put it back in the drawer, unzipped a pocket on his good leg, put the hypo-spray unit and the other tube in his pocket, and zipped it up.

He moved over to the console and tapped a few buttons, the console lit up as sensors came to life, and the wall melted into a vid screen:

GAMMA II – ENVIRONMENTAL AND
CLIMATOLOGICAL RESEARCH STATION

ESTABLISHED SEPTEMBER 15, 2273,
CAPTAIN REBECCA MACPHERSON –
GEOPHYSICAL SCIENTIST, AND
OPERATIONALCOMMANDER

EARTH ALLIANCE STATION 132 – CREW
COMPLIMENT 8

"What the hell!" His fog clearing some, memory starting to return, he tapped a few more keys. The computer sensed him, and the screen changed:

COMMANDER DANIEL BOWERS
BORN FEBURARY 23, 2231

SAN DIEGO, CALIFORNIA, NORTH
AMERICAN CONTINENT, EARTH, SOL
SYSTEM

MISSING IN ACTION 2263, CONFIRMED
DEAD 2264

ENTERED EARTH SCIENCE ACADEMY
IN 2249, STUDIES INCLUDED PLANETARY
ENVIRONMENTAL SCIENCES, CRIMINAL
INVESTIGATION

LOST ON A DEEP SPACE RESEARCH MISSON
NEAR GAMMA II ON AUGUST 15, 2263

"I'm. . . dead?"

"My files are incomplete per that inquiry, Sir," a female voice replied.

Bowers jumped, "Who said that?"

"I am the *Gamma II* Science and Research Station, Sir."

"Who, what, where is your crew?"

"A crew of six left to investigate Waterman Crater eight hours ago, investigating seismic anomalies, and an atmospheric storm on the far side of the planet. I have had no contact with the mission crew or Earth and Mars for over six hours due to the electromagnetic pulse from the *Triton Sun,* five hours earlier."

His head started to throb again with this new information and the pain meds wearing off, he laid down on one of the medical beds and fell asleep. A green light started to wash over him.

"Sir, I would not sleep right now, you have a concussion, Sir?" the Computer explained.

Bowers mumbles, "Jessie, Jessie. . ."

He did not know how long he had slept, not slept but at least rested some, he sat up, and swung his legs to one side, now feeling no more pain, but his mind was still fuzzy.

"Good evening, Commander Bowers. How did you sleep?" the Computer asked.

"I slept better than I ever. . ." Bower started and then remembered the conversation with the Computer earlier.

"A fresh uniform, Sir? You will find one here?" the Computer asked as a section of the wall near him slid open, revealing a locker with fresh uniforms, blue, green, and yellow. He grabbed a blue one and started removing his old, tattered brown flight suit, "First, tell me, how did you recognize me? Comp. . . you stated I was dead?"

"Presumed dead, Sir. I ran a scan as you slept, matched your DNA to the copy on file, and then repaired your wounds. You have been asleep for about nine hours."

He continued changing into a fresh jumpsuit, "How could I be alive if your file. . . stated I was dead?"

"Again, presumed dead, Sir. You have been missing for ten years. After the scan, I confirmed who you were, and updated my files." The computer answered.

"Thank you, I think?"

A small square sink emerged from the wall, three squared around. A slit opened and a stream of water flowed out. He washed his face, and a small section of the wall above the sink melted into a mirror, "You shaved me?"

"You looked a bit worse for wear, Sir."

"What else did you. . ." running his hands over his body, "Never mind?" And he finished cleaning up, and placed a pocketknife from his old suit into his new one, in a lower pocket, "You stated, you lost contact with the crew six hours ago and I have been sleeping for nine hours, so they have been missing over fifteen hours?"

"Yes, Sir, fifteen point, one three seven to be precise."

Picking a towel up from the top shelf of the locker, drying his face and hands, and looked back into the mirror, *I look good for forty, ten years and not a day older,* he told himself, "With your systems back online, do you have any readings from Captain Macpherson and her crew?"

"No, Sir. I cannot even locate the ship's beacon."

"And still no contact with Earth or Mars?"

"Correct, Sir, may I ask what all you remember, since your death?"

Bowers chuckled as he fell back in the chair, "My death? Nothing, only walking through the desert, bits and pieces coming back, now, slowly, after reading my life story, but mostly still a blank."

"Parts of my data are missing too, Sir."

"Looks like we're in the same boat, *Gamma*."

"Boat. . . *Gamma*. . . Sir?"

"Boat, as in we both have pieces missing from our databanks. *Gamma*, which is this station's name, correct?"

"Correct, but the crew always called me, Computer."

"My Father, before his passing, a brilliant Computer Engineer, told me, 'A Computer is like a lady, she has more intelligence than you or any man if programmed correctly, so treat her right, and she will treat you right.' And I hope you accept that?"

"Yes, Sir," *Gamma* answered.

"So, let's start with finding out what happened to Macpherson and her crew. Show me a map to Command?"

"Out the door, proceed to your right, and walk to the end of the corridor," *Gamma* said as the medical door slid open.

This new jumpsuit felt good, and better than his old one. *Earth finally got a good tailor,* he thought.

Above the door, COMMAND in red, but it remained closed, he touched the pad, but nothing, "*Gamma*, the door is not opening."

"A moment, Sir, still bringing my systems back online and re-pressurizing the room."

"Why pressurize, when the pressure and air outside is that of Earth?" Bowers questioned.

"During my reboot, the structure defaults to normal conditions on this planet, even the interior of the dome, something my programmers added. It is Earth's normal for two hundred of the four hundred fifty days of this planet's rotational cycle around *Triton*. When it is closer to the *Triton Sun*, the air becomes filled with carbon dioxide that is seventy atmospheres heavier than that of Earth," *Gamma* explained, "In twenty days, the air will change back to carbon dioxide, all transpiring within a forty-eight-hour period."

Bowers thought for a moment, "Even with the heat of the *Triton* Sun and the dead world out there, there is no way that could happen in forty-eight hours," pointing over his shoulder with his thumb.

"That is my normal boot procedure, Sir."

"Then we have less than twenty days to find Macpherson and her crew."

The door slid open to a dark room. Only a few lights on the center console were active, "Yes, Sir."

Command was not large, could hold about six comfortably, only two consoles, one in the center, similar to the med bay, but twice the size, and a second one across the room under the center window, "Since it's just the two of us, *Gamma*, Bowers will do fine."

"Yes, Sir—Bowers."

He tapped a few places on the console. More lights activate in the room and outside. He could now see out the three large windows that encircle the room. He shifted up to the second console and noticed that it was now dusk outside. Tapped more, he found the station's status report: *normal oxygen levels and food stores in good condition.* "*Gamma*, I read a crew compliment of eight assigned here?"

"Yes, Sir, eight assigned, Bowers."

"Then, why are there enough food stores for over two hundred?"

"No data to account. The crew is eight for two hundred days."

This didn't add up. How could there be this many food stores for a crew of two hundred, but only an active crew of eight? "Other than your memory loss, can you report any problems with the station?"

"No, the *Gamma II* station is working properly, Sir."

"Are you able to find the Captain's last log entry before the crew left? And can your sensors locate the remaining crew?"

"I have found Captain Macpherson's last log entry," *Gamma* advised.

"Play, please?"

He looked up as the window above the console darkened and melted into a vid screen with Captain Rebecca Macpherson in a set of quarters at a console----Irish, in her late thirties, with shoulder-length red hair, and wearing a blue jumpsuit. She had four gold stripes around her sleeves, and on her right arm that was lying on the console, *she looked familiar*, he thought.

"We have been reading high seismic activity, over ten on the Richter scale on the far side of the planet, near Waterman Crater, one of the largest on this planet. There is also a magnetic storm entering the area. A crew of five and I will be setting out in a few hours to study the area before the storm becomes too heavy for our sensors. Chief Engineer Adams and Medical Technician, Ensign Swanson will stay behind, Captain Rebecca Macpherson reporting." The screen dissolved back to black, and then back to the desert outside.

"Sounds like a normal report, but what happened to Swanson and Adams?"

"No data at this time," *Gamma* answered.

"Show me their flight path, please?" The window again melted, but this time into a digital representation of the station and the planet with an arc of the shuttle, a dotted yellow line moved from the station over the planet's north pole and down without touching again, "Your data ends there?"

"Yes, Bowers."

"Is there a report where Adams was last?"

"Engin—"

The alarm rang out, and red lights flooded the room. "Show me the path to Engineering," Bowers ordered.

A yellow dotted line begins to run from the central hub in Command down the third leg of the habitat on the console. He darted out of Command after reviewing the map. He ran down the corridor, tracing the map from the screen in his head, turning left at the end of the corridor, and stopped swiftly at the door of Engineering.

Above the door, ENGINEERING in red, finally the door opened. There was smoke everywhere; alarms continued ringing out and red lights flashing.

"Kill the alarms and turn on the vents!" The red light and alarms stopped. Vents pull the smoke from the room, there was a pipe spraying steam near the door, Bowers opened a panel and turns a red spiral knob, and the steam slows, then stopped, "Report Gamma?"

"Chief Adams, second level, near the center console," *Gamma* answered.

He looked around quickly, rang up the ramp to the second level, and looked over the console. Chief Adams, Commander, three gold stripes, late sixties, heavyset man, balding, lying on his belly. He turned him over. A large bruise on his forehead above his right eye, and he was wearing a yellow jumpsuit and tool belt. "Adams!" But no response. "*Gamma*, is he alive?"

"Yes, Sir."

Bowers picked up the heavyset man, pulling Adam's left arm over his shoulder, dragged him down the ramp and out of Engineering to the medical bay, and laid him on one of the beds, "Complete scan, please, *Gamma*?"

The green light started, "Contusion to his right optical nerve, cerebral hemorrhaging, he will be out for several hours until the swelling reduces," *Gamma* reported.

"Any sensor reports of Swanson?"

"No, Sir."

Bowers sat at the console, looking across the room, as the green light continued, "What the hell were you doing?"

TWENTY-FOUR HOURS EARLIER

The shuttle lifted gently off the north pad of the *Gamma II* research station, about five meters long, five meters high, rectangular, curving up into a squared back, with two flat elongated tubes along the bottom, drive pods.

The shuttle had one large window along the front, divided into three viewports, two smaller ones on each side of the shuttle, one being inside the hatch, causing a limited view, and rose slowly, with a green light underneath, and hovers up and over the dome toward the north.

Captain Macpherson and Lieutenant Calvin sit in the front compartment, four large back swivel chairs and the console arcs around from behind the pilot's chair on the left, up and around the front compartment. It continues around and back behind the command chair, on the right, and a small panel between both chairs, two squared panels on the ceiling above the walkway between the chairs.

Lieutenant John Calvin, a young African American in his late twenties, has short black hair, wearing a blue jumpsuit, and two gold stripes, slowly tapping on the console, piloting the shuttle, as the Sun is slowly setting.

"The days are getting shorter, Captain," Calvin suggested.

"Yes," Macpherson replied without looking up from her console.

A green light flashed, and they heard three quick chirps, "Sensors are detecting something on the surface, Ma'am."

Macpherson looked up from her console and tapped a few times on the center. Four lights shine out and down onto the ground ahead of them. The bright white light changed to blue, orange, and finally green.

"Sensors are not registering, but something was down there," Calvin said.

"Then nothing to report."

"Yes, Ma'am. On to Waterman Crater."

Lieutenant Katherine Walker-Swanson entered from the back compartment, mid-twenties, with short blond hair around her ears, blue jumpsuits, two gold stripes, bright green eyes, and a wedding band. She hands a small white electronic screen to Macpherson.

"So, how was your honeymoon with Theresa?" Macpherson asked as she took the screen.

Walker-Swanson smiles and spotted Calvin's facial expressions. Rolling his eyes, snickering, and hoping she did not see him, "Not long enough!"

"Doctor Mabuto stated she had to stay behind, he is the senior medical officer and was coming along," Macpherson replied.

"The quakes on this side of the planet are increasing, and the storm is intensifying," Walker-Swanson explained, hoping to change the subject.

Macpherson looked over the screen, "Is Hitchcock's equipment ready?"

"Commander Hitchcock stated, adamantly, that he will need three hours to set up and calibrate," Walker-Swanson replied as she sat down in the chair behind command.

"He has an hour, so he better be ready."

A lightning bolt struck the lower drive pod, near the rear, and rocked the shuttle from side to side. Alarms sounded and red lights started flashing.

Calvin tries feverishly to compensate and settles the shuttle some, "Sorry, Cap! Missed that bolt."

Macpherson glared at him. He knew that she did not accept that slang word for her rank and she helped him stabilize the shuttle from her console.

The shuttle jerked again, this time forward. Smoke started coming from the ceiling panels in front and above. The shuttle rocketed across the sky, black smoke trailing beneath it, from one of the drive pods, and slammed hard into the floor of the crater. The storm continued raging on, fiercely, with heavy lightning and sand everywhere blowing all around.

Calvin was slumped over the pilot's console; Walker-Swanson was lying on the floor, smoke and sand poured into the compartment, red lights flashing, and alarms still ringing out. Macpherson was nowhere to be seen. Where she was sitting was now a large hole in the observation window above where she was sitting. The fierce wind and whistling were still blowing through the compartment.

The door between the two compartments was being forced open, Doctor Remy Mabuto, a dark-skinned South African, in his sixties. Commander, wearing a white medical jacket with two pockets over his green jumpsuit, a small set of tools, and a penlight in one of the front pockets, he has a small amount of gray around his head, and wearing small gold-framed reading glasses, which are hanging from a gold chain around his neck.

He was forcing the door open between the two compartments, with the help of a young blonde, Thomas Mitchell. Technician Lieutenant, two gold stripes, early twenties, Australian, and a wizard with electronics, the station's junior engineer, yellow jumpsuit, and tool belt, helping the Doctor.

"Push, Thomas," Mabuto yelled with his soft-spoken and hard Afrikaner accent with British-speaking tones. Mabuto leaned down next to Walker-Swanson, and she moaned, and slowly shifted, "Easy, Kathy, take it easy, you will be all right."

"What happened?" Walker-Swanson asked as he helped her up into the chair behind command, then shifted over to Calvin, checking his pulse along the back of his neck, then looked back down at her, and shook his head, mouthing, "No, no, no."

"Mitchell, sit rep!" she ordered.

Mitchell pulls Calvin's lifeless body from the pilot's chair and lays him on the deck, taps a few buttons, and lights come on, "Primary systems are down, probably due to the magnetic storm."

"How's the back, Doc?" Walker-Swanson asked.

"In better shape than up here."

"We need to find out how we are doing and where the Captain is. Mitchell, you check out the ship, the Doctor and I will look for the Captain out there." She said as they glanced through the opening.

"What about Calvin, Lieutenant?" Mitchell asked.

"Put him in the back for now, out of the way," she answers, as she tries to stand, but sways and nearly drops back down. The Doctor catches her.

"You are not going anywhere yet, Lieutenant," Mabuto said in a fatherly way, helping her back into the chair, "Not till I can check you out, fully. Thomas takes Calvin's body to the back and starts on the ship." Mitchell drags Calvin's lifeless body to the back.

Mabuto turned the command chair around and sat. With his penlight checked her eyes, then with his hands, slowly moved her head and neck. She winced, "You may have a slight concussion, so take it easy till we get back to the station."

"Doctor's orders?" she replied mocking him.

He put his hand on her shoulder, "You need to be in one piece when you see your wife again, or I will never hear the end of it," he said smiling, then winked and then returned to the back.

Walker-Swanson tried again to stand once more, dizzy, swaying, and fell back catching herself with the chair, as more lights and panels lit up.

Mitchell called out over the COM, "Partial power restored, sensors are my next task."

Walker-Swanson leaned forward, and tapped the COM, "How is Hitchcock?"

The Doctor replied slowly over the COM, "Unconscious, he was slammed into the bulkhead."

"And his equipment?"

"Not sure yet, LT," Mitchell replied.

Captain Macpherson lays face down on the desert floor, her left leg twisted up and under the other. As the storm continued overhead, she woke and rolled over slowly, shifting her twisted leg, and cringing with pain. She looked around, but with the storm, she could barely see a few meters in front of her.

She pulled a small cylinder from her right shoulder pocket, "Shuttle Copernicus, can you read me?" but there was no reply, only static. Then she pulled a long tube from her right leg pocket, a flashlight, and flashed it around over the area, still not able to see. The sandstorm was too fierce.

She ripped off part of her left sleeve, a makeshift bandana, and tied it around her head covering her nose and mouth, and tried standing. She knew her as was broken, she leaned against a large boulder which was next to her and wondered if that was how she broke her leg. She repositioned and stood against the large boulder, and tried her COM again, but still only static.

Mitchell came forward with a small silver toolbox, placed it in the command chair, and pulled out a small metal-framed pistol with a long cylindrical tube connected. He sprayed a stream of clear gel around the hole, quickly covering the jagged edges, then out in circles toward the center. The gel slowly hardened back into a sheet of glass, and the whistling stopped, "Sensors are back online, but useless in this storm, LT."

Walker-Swanson nodded, "How many environmental suits?"

"Two complete, the other two were damaged in the crash."

"Get them ready for me and the Doctor. "We're going after the Captain," She stood with help from the bulkhead and sat in the pilot's chair, looking over the sensors, "I see an opening in about two minutes," and started toward the back compartment. Mitchell collected the pistol and toolbox and followed her out.

The back compartment, with double sliding doors in the far rear to another compartment, large cargo crates and circular high plastic crates, with an elongated table seating six, two high back chairs on each side, and one on each end. Two twin stacked bunks on either side of the room, with the table in between, Calvin's lifeless body was now lying on one of the lower bunks with a sheet over his head. An eight-stacked shelf unit, with mesh bindings for holding more equipment back near the hatch, the Doctor was on the other side of the room checking on Hitchcock, who was lying on the top bunk.

Commander Robert Hitchcock, late forties, with salt and peppered hair a thin black mustache, and a sling across his chest and right arm, and wearing a blue jumpsuit.

"How is he, Doc?" Walker-Swanson asked as she slowly walked over, using the table for support, and reaching out toward the Doctor.

"The same."

Mitchell carried two suits from the back and dropped them on the table, "Ready, LT."

Macpherson yelled but could not even hear her own voice over the storm, and as if the storm had heard her, it settled. She pulled a set of small binoculars from her right leg pocket. Inside the binoculars, two circles rotated looking over the plateau, she moved it from left to right, but still too hard to see. Data started scrolling down her right display, but not reporting accurately, she placed it back into her pocket and straightened up, feeling the pain cascading through her broken leg, and positioned herself where she had landed and started walking, believing it to be the best way back to the shuttle.

Lightning cracked around her. Adjusting her makeshift bandanna, she started her long journey back, limping slowly, but only a few steps, and stopped, he good foot felt the edge of the cliff, and realized she was on the rim of the crater. Waterman Crater and saw the shuttle below, only a few meters ahead. She looked around for a way down and found one, a few centimeters to her right, and continued.

The shuttle's hatch closed. Doctor Mabuto and Walker-Swanson were outside now, Walker-Swanson looking over a screen in her hands, and moving it slowly from right to left, "It's detecting a signal about fifteen meters, in that direction." Walker-Swanson explained now wearing a blue environmental suit, and pointed across the Doctor's chest, who was in a green environmental suit, "Mitchell, keep working on the shuttle and find out what brought us down, I don't think it was just the wind."

"Aye, LT."

They headed out across the crater floor toward the rim, as the wind picked up again, and became too hard to see for a moment.

"My scanner states, except for the high winds, we do not need the suits, but I would not remove them because of the dust," the Doctor suggested reading his screen.

"Yes."

The storm raged on high above them, and Mabuto's screen beeped. He tapped, "The scanner detects a life form, and it is moving toward us."

She looked over at him with puzzlement, "The Captain may be all right, then?"

"Yes---- here!" She pointed ahead of them, and they ran.

Macpherson reached the crater floor, checked with her binoculars again, and saw two figures moving toward her, and picked up the pace, feeling the pain more, knowing there was no life on this planet, but her crew. She now can see, running more, but no use with her broken leg, she tripped and fell.

The Doctor rushed up to her, catching her before slamming into the ground, "I got you, Bekka."

"Thought we lost you, Ma'am," Walker-Swanson said.

"Water?" Macpherson asked with a hoarse voice.

Mabuto pulled a small canteen that was hanging on his belt, removed the cap, and helped her drink, "Slowly, slowly, not too fast."

Fighting to gain her voice, "Report, Lieutenant."

Walker-Swanson hesitated at first, and Macpherson looked directly at her, waiting for an answer, "Shuttle down, Mitchell on repairs, Hitchcock unconscious, and Calvin. . . Calvin is dead, Ma'am."

Macpherson sighed, hearing the news of Calvin, the first crew member she had ever lost under her Command. She got up fast with the Doctor's help, "How far is the shuttle?"

"About fifteen meters." Walker-Swanson points back in the direction they came.

"We better get moving."

Catching her again she fell forward, not waiting for either of them or help, "You are not going anywhere till I brace that leg, Bekka," Doctor Mabuto ordered.

"Yes, Remy."

Mabuto swung an oversized backpack that was on his back, pulling out a long rectangular brace with two black straps connected on one side, to brace her leg. He placed the frame under and fixed one strap under and the other over her upper thigh, pulling her leg fully. As he closed the final strap around her ankle, she let out a scream, then he pulled out a hypo-spray and jabbed it into her upper thigh, a hissing sound, and they helped her up, leaning on the Doctor, they headed off.

"Mitchell, we're back with the Captain. Open up," Walker-Swanson ordered over the COM.

The hatch slowly rose. The Doctor and the Captain enter first, then Walker-Swanson. The hatch closed. The Doctor sat the Captain at the table, and they both removed their helmets.

Macpherson looks around for Mitchell, "Report Mister?"

Mitchell entered from the front compartment, "An electromagnetic pulse from a solar flare hit, we were out for about five hours."

"Have you contacted the station?" Macpherson asked.

"Not in this storm, Ma'am. Maybe in six hours once sensors are back online, and the storm has passed." Mitchell answered.

Macpherson nodded.

"Six hours, I order sleep for everyone," the Doctor ordered.

"Yes, Sir," all replied.

Macpherson awoke and looked around seeing all but Mitchell sleeping, proceeded slowly with her limp to the front compartment, and found Mitchell lying on his back, working under the console.

"How are we doing?" she asked, slowly leaning, and dropping into the chair behind command.

"We should be able to contact the station in about twenty minutes. Once I get this final relay in place." Mitchell answered and they heard a snapping sound as the breaker connected, as he connected both cables.

"Good, I didn't see Calvin's body when I woke up?"

"I put him in a body bag before you'll got back from your walkabout, and then put him in the back storage," he answered, with his slight Australian accent coming out.

The Doctor joined them, "Good morning."

"Is it morning?" Macpherson questioned.

"Well, the Sun will be up in about a half hour."

Mitchell stood and shifted into the pilot's chair. "Starting the engines," He tapped a few buttons, lights in the front compartment brightened, and they could hear the engines slowly roaring, "Can you cycle the matter-antimatter cells, Captain?"

Macpherson shifted slowly to the command chair and reached over her right shoulder, tapping a few buttons. The engine sound doubled and then settled, and more lights on the consoles appeared.

"Good job, Mitchell. So how soon till we can launch?" she asked.

"Not long, Captain," he replied, exiting the front compartment.

"How is your leg feeling?" Doctor Mabuto asked.

"I have more feeling and less pain, is that good?"

Walker-Swanson entered, yawning, "Mitchell says we're ready to get underway."

"I would not worry; we have not been gone that long that she will miss her new bride. Please take the pilot's chair?" Macpherson said jokingly.

Walker-Swanson glared at her. She was getting tired of all their comments, and sat, "Ha, ha."

Macpherson and Mabuto just smiled.

Mitchell called out over the COM, "Captain, you can contact the station now."

Macpherson pressed the COM above the center panel. "Thank you, Mitchell," Then reached up higher and pressed another button on the forward console, "Macpherson to *Gamma II*, please reply." There was nothing, no reply.

"Macpherson to *Gamma II*, please reply," Still nothing, She pressed the COM again, "Mitchell, you sure we're transmitting?"

Over the COM, "Aye, Ma'am, we are transmitting, But I will go outside and check the antenna, report shortly," Mitchell answered.

"The electromagnetic pulse from the flare could have knocked out the station, as it did us," Walker-Swanson suggested.

"Let's hope it's that or the antenna," Mabuto offered as he moved to the back compartment, "I should check on Hitchcock before we launch."

Mitchell, now outside and near the back of the shuttle, without an environmental suit, the wind was calm, he placed a small kit on the narrow ledge near three flat closed panels embedded into the bulkhead and took out a screen, opened one of the three panels. Pressed on the center one with his palm, pushing gently, it dropped back inside, and sided up, leaving an edge for him to tap closed. Takes out a small tool from his kit, a straight piece of glass, square shape, about the length of a pencil, and slides it in and out slowly, it starts to glow and then faster, changing from clear to orange and finally red. He moves it up and down and then holds it over the screen, tapping a few times, and then looks over the screen.

Pulls a small cylinder from his pocket, "Captain, the antenna is working properly."

"Understood, it must be the station. Get back inside, we're heading back," Macpherson said over the COM.

"Yes, Ma'am," he answered as he put the rod and screen back into his kit and pressed the edge of the panel. It slowly lowered and sealed back into the bulkhead, he touched the panel on the side hatch and entered.

He placed the kit back into a rack near the hatch, behind a few mesh straps, and touched the COM button, "All set, Captain, launch when ready."

"Hold on, everyone, could be a bumpy ride," Walker-Swanson advised.

The shuttle rose slowly and sluggishly off the plateau, bolting back and forth, flying off, still with black smoke from one of the drive pods, rocking from side to side, off over the crater's rim, as the Sun rose ahead of them with the storm finally settling.

Bowers was going over data in Engineering at the center console, "*Gamma,* do you understand this subroutine Adams placed in your main command line functions?"

"The algorithm does not match my system code, Bowers."

Bowers taps a few buttons and brings up Adams's service record:

EARL G. ADAMS, BORN 2205—MARE
ACIDALIUM, MARS—STUDIED
ENGINEERING AT MARS ACADAMY

BEFORE ENTERING EARTH ALLIANCE
ENGINEERING GROUP—AFTER THE MARS
COLONY RESISTANCE MOVEMENT. ASSIGN
TO EARTH, THEN GAMMA II, SHORTLY
AFTER THE SUDDEN DEATH OF THE
PRIMARY ENGINEER, CAUFIELD.

"*Gamma,* do you have any more information on Caulfield and his mysterious death?"

"That information is missing from my data files," *Gamma* replied, "I will need a full download of new information after we can link with Earth or Mars."

Bowers was not sure what to think about this and let out a heavy sigh.

"Bowers, my sensors are now reading the shuttle returning and will be touching down shortly."

"Maybe, we'll get some answers now," Bowers commented leaving Engineering.

Walker-Swanson lowered the battered shuttle over the complex toward the pad at the end of the fourth leg of the hub. The shuttle landed with a loud thud, "Sorry."

"*Gamma II*, are you reading me?" Macpherson asked over the COM.

"Yes, Captain, I am here," *Gamma* replied.

"Sit rep?"

"Over thirty percent of my memory banks are corrupted due to the EM pulse, Chief Adams is unconscious after complications due to sabotage, and Ensign Swanson is still missing, . . . and Commander Bowers is helping with my repairs," *Gamma* reported.

Macpherson paused, hearing his name, but he was dead.

Walker-Swanson looked over at her with confusion and concern toward her wife.

"Commander Bowers?" Macpherson questioned.

"Yes, Ma'am, I will let him explain."

"This *will* be good," Macpherson said.

"Who's Commander Bowers?" Walker-Swanson asked.

"He *was* a leading Planetary Environmental Scientist over ten years ago and lost in this quadrant on one of the first research missions to the *Triton* system, *was* declared missing in action, and dead," Macpherson explained.

Each looked at each other stunned as to how. Macpherson wonders how and why now. She had not seen or talked to him since the Mars Riots.

Macpherson and Walker-Swanson move toward the back compartment. Macpherson limped over toward the Doctor, who was still near Hitchcock. Walker-Swanson moved back near the hatch and opened it, Mitchell was nowhere to be seen.

"The computer states you have an additional patient in the med bay----Chief Adams." She hobbles over toward the hatch. "and oh yes, we have a visitor. . . *Commander Bowers.*"

The Doctor's eyes widen. He had missed his old friend, Mitchell finally emerged from the back storage with a stretcher, closed the double doors behind him, and placed it on the floor near the bunk, he and the Doctor placed Hitchcock on the stretcher, and picked him up, and they all head out, as Walker-Swanson assist Macpherson letting her lean on her.

The crew continued toward the structure, Walker-Swanson still helping Macpherson, allowing her to lean on her, followed by the Doctor and Mitchell. The large outer bay door lowered slowly down onto the pad.

Bowers was leaning against a few cargo crates near the opening.

"He has not aged a day," the Doctor whispered under his breath, hoping no one heard him. Macpherson glanced over at the Doctor and then back at Bowers.

"Welcome home, Captain," Bowers called out.

"Where the hell did you come from?" She asked, limping up the ramp on her own now.

"Your guess is as good as mine," Bowers answered stepping closer to her.

Mitchell and the Doctor preceded into the station with a still unconscious Hitchcock, the Doctor watching him, and smiled. Walker-Swanson ran and tackled Bowers hard, knocking him to the deck, "Where the hell is my wife and what have you done with her, asshole!"

Falling back and struggling, Bowers tries to hold her off.

Macpherson hobbles down and half-leans, grabbing her, "That's enough, Lieutenant!" pulling her off, "Get to Command and fix the computer!" Macpherson ordered.   Walker-Swanson shot a harsh look back at Bowers and stormed off.

Macpherson offered her hand and helped him to his feet, "So what's been going on here?"

"*Gamma* and I are still trying to figure that out."

"Gamma?"

Bowers stood, "Well, it was just me and the station, it was only right to give her a name."

"So, what can you tell me, and where the hell have you been?"

"I can answer most of that in Engineering," he replied with his hand out for her to lead. She continued and he followed.

The oversized bay door closed slowly behind them.

"After I arrived, I learned where I was from *Gamma's* files, and watching your log, I found Chief Adams here, unconscious, trying to destroy the station with a new subroutine," he explained and brought up the subroutine.

Macpherson pulled a chair up from behind them, and read it, "I have not seen this before; Walker-Swanson will have to look it over, she is our Computer Specialist, and what about you?" Leaning back in the chair, "Where the hell did you come from?"

Throwing his hands up, leaning back against the side console, "Your guess is as good as mine. I wish I knew. . . All I do remember is walking through the desert out there with one hell of a headache, and according to *Gamma*, once her redundant systems recognized me, after the pulse. I knew who I was and where I was, but nothing more," Bowers explained.

"But it's been over ten years!"

Bowers just nods.

"And I take it, you and the Doctor have a history?" She had heard the Doctor and agreed.

"He was the medical officer assigned to the ship on the original research mission and an old family friend."

"So, you found the station offline, Adams trying to sabotage it, and Swanson is still missing?"

"Yep, except for a few doors that opened, the station was dead, and I started looking over *Gamma's* files, learning of your crew and your mission here and to the crater. At first, *Gamma* could not locate either Adams or Swanson but as her sensors came back online, alarms rang out. We found Adams here, and I took him to the med bay, found this subroutine, and then *Gamma* told me you all were back," he summarized.

"And you still remember nothing before all that?"

Before he could answer, Walker-Swanson entered, "Captain, I have been able to recover about twenty percent of the computer's data and will need a fresh download for the rest. And now with your permission, I wish to find my wife!" She turned to leave.

"No!" Macpherson commanded as she stood and hobbled down the ramp, "You are too emotional. Commander Bowers and I will continue the search."

"You're listening to this stranger, now? How do you know he is who he says he is?"

Macpherson moved closer, "He is, who I say he is because he was one of my instructors at Command College and my Commanding officer during the Mars Riots. Well, you were still in high school. Now return to Command and continue with *Gamma's* files!"

"*Gamm—*"

Pointing at the door, "The damn computer, now go!"

"So, I did recognize you on the screen when I watched your log," Bowers commented as she turned back.

"Yes, and the Doctor was right, you have not aged a day since you went missing."

He nods again.

"And how long have you known the good Doctor?" Macpherson asked, sitting back down.

Bowers giggled and thought back, "It's a long story, he married my parents."

Macpherson glared back at him, with shock, "How old is Remy?"

"God only knows. . . but I must tell you first, I am the youngest of four kids and the only son, my parents were both married before, and both were in their late fifties when I was born. Mom met Remy well on a dig in South Africa, assigned there by the World Government in relief efforts, she was brought into the area after the Consolidation of Africa in 2225, once it became a single government. Mom was a consultant on the Archeology of Africa, and Dad, a Computer Engineer, helped the government update its systems. Mom had met Remy after an accident at a dig; he was working as a Doctor, teaching, and finishing his studies at Stellenbosch University, in both Medicine and Ministry. Six months later, he married my parents and has been an uncle, mentor, and friend ever since."

"Wow!" Macpherson answered with her eyes wide and shaking her head.

"Yeah, most have that reaction when I explain my family relationship to Remy, and I take it he married the Swanson, too?"

Macpherson nodded, taking it all in, "Captain, you and Commander Bowers should check out the pumping station, my sensors are reporting a blockage in the moon pool, now that Lieutenant Walker-Swanson has repaired them, and I am back online more," *Gamma* informed them.

"Yes, *Gamma*," both answered.

"This way, I don't think you have seen the pumping station."

Bowers chuckled, "Only from the exterior," softly under his breath.

They exited Engineering, hurrying down the long corridor, turning left, and down another one, and up to an oversized door like the outer bay door, as it was already sliding open, he found a room full of hydroponics, with a large glass ceiling.

Macpherson leads the way to the center of the room, and both notice a body in the pool, with an arm caught in one of the pumps, hearing a grinding noise. Bowers took off, jumped in, and turned over the young woman's body.

"Swanson!" Macpherson yelled and limped-ran up to the pool, trying to help. Bowers worked Swanson's arm out of the pipe, "*Gamma!* Notify Doctor Mabuto, fast," Macpherson ordered.

Bowers pulled Ensign Swanson out of the water. Ensign Theresa Swanson, early twenties, on her first medical assignment out of the academy, with brown hair down just past her shoulders, and like the Doctor, wearing a green jumpsuit, with a single gold stripe.

Mabuto and Mitchell entered carrying the stretcher and followed by Walker-Swanson, with fury on her face toward Bowers, pushing him out of the way and back into the pool.

She helped Mitchell and Mabuto get her wife on the stretcher, "How is she, Doc?"

"Unconscious. I will know more once we get her back to the medical bay," Mitchell, Mabuto, and Walker-Swanson carry Swanson out.

Bowers sits on the edge of the pool, looking at Macpherson. Who hands him a towel from a nearby table.

Mitchell now working in Engineering, Bowers joined him, "Have you figured anything out?"

Tapping a few buttons, not looking up at him almost ignoring him, "Not yet, Sir. It's a tricky routine. Kathy may do better with it, than I."

"Can you tell when it was placed in the system and what it does?"

"No, but it was entered five days into activation of the station after *our* arrival."

"Keep working on it, and let the Captain and I know what you find, please?"

Mitchell paused, hearing him say please, then looked up, never hearing an officer use it, and with sincerity, "Yes, Sir," he replied.

Bowers returned to the medical bay, the Doctor was working at the console, Chief Adams was still lying on the far bed, Hitchcock on the middle one, and Swanson was now sitting up, leaning against her wife, on the third, with a cast over her arm and hand.

Macpherson was standing near them, and waved him over, "Commander Daniel Bowers, this is Ensign Theresa Swanson, our last missing crew member."

"Good to meet you, Ensign," Bowers said as he stepped up near them.

"Swanson has been telling us that before the EM pulse, she found Chief Adams in Engineering, near the core, and they struggled, next you were pulling her out of the pool," Macpherson explained.

"Only thing I can think of, was Chief Adams knocked you out, put you in the pool to drown you, so it would look like an accident, and then went back to Engineering and was about to run the program. The EM pulse knocked everything out, suspending all systems until I turned

Gamma back on. As the systems came back online, fires in Engineering must have set the alarms off," he concluded.

The Doctor walked over to Chief Adams, "People, I have some new information on Chief Adams's condition." Macpherson and Bowers join him, "I found this implanted in the back of his neck, near his medulla oblongata," as he tossed a small disk to Bowers, a three-centimeter-in-diameter circle, with a smaller circle inside the larger disk with a bright red light flashing.

"Controlled?" Bowers asked.

"I believe so," the Doctor answered pointing at the small disk, now in Bowers's hand, "I believe that is what overloaded Chief Adams's brain and caused him to crack his head on the console, when he fell, an electrical shock overloaded his brain. The only reason I can see why he is still unconscious," Doctor Mabuto explained.

Macpherson and Bowers look at each other, "Are you saying we have a spy among us, Doctor?" Walker-Swanson asked looking at Bowers as she joined them.

"I cannot answer that Lieutenant," the Doctor replied.

Walker-Swanson and the Doctor both look at Macpherson.

"Spies are out of my league Doc," Macpherson answered.

"I guess, you have a mystery on your hands, Dan. As I recall, you were one of the best investigators ten years ago," the Doctor reminded him.

Bowers lets out a heavy sigh.

The door slid open and all turned, as Mitchell entered, "Doc, did you take Calvin's body from the shuttle?"

"No, I have not, is there something wrong, Thomas?"

Mitchell looked from the Doctor to the Captain, "Ma'am, I must report Calvin's body. . . is missing. I went back to the shuttle to bring him to cool storage, but he was not there."

"What do you mean he was *not* there?" she asked.

"Ma'am, his body was not in the shuttle. The body bag was there that I placed him in, but it was open as if he climbed out!"

Macpherson looked at Bowers, "We have a spy, a dead body walking around, and a subroutine in our system, which we have no idea what it does. What else could go wrong? I guess, a welcome back is out of the question, now?"

Bowers sat at a console in a set of quarters, contemplating over the small disk device, which Mabuto found in Chief Adams's brain.

"*Gamma,* can you display my last mission report before I was placed MIA and then declared dead?"

"I am sorry, Bowers, without an Uplink to Earth, I cannot comply."

"Then we're all flying blind."

The door chimed, "Come . . ." He swiveled around, and saw Calvin standing there, eyes glowing red, "Commander Daniel Bowers," an Ancient and powerful voice spoke, and Bowers noticed that Calvin's mouth was not moving, "Get off my planet!" and then he raised his right arm, red bolts flashed from his fingertips, encircling Bowers. The console exploded, fire, and smoke everywhere. The explosion tossed Bowers across the room, bouncing him off the bed and slamming him onto the floor, on his back. Calvin vanished.

"Commander Bowers?" *Gamma* asked.

Bowers laid there, motionlessly on the floor with his eyes wide open, his eyes then flashed white, as alarms sounded and red lights flashed.

CHAPTER TWO

TERRA FERRMA

Earth 2260

ALONG A DUSTY DIRT ROAD on a blistering hot summer day, in mid-August, temperatures reaching as high as one hundred and ten degrees in the shade, with the heat of the Sun, steaming off the blacktop.

Waves crash on the sandy beach and return into the ocean. Three young boys sit on a clay wall, fishing, giggling, and drinking cold sodas, some distance down the beach there is a group of people sitting at a picnic table, a few meters behind them, barbequing, and talking, enjoying their sunny summer day. Two women in their twenties jog, converse, and giggle, enjoying a hot summer day with a cool breeze from the gulf winds, in this small sleepy Texas beach town.

Daniel Bowers walked slowly along the beach, a short way down from the boys, wearing an oversized white-and-black pair of swim trunks, which reached down around and past his knees, and gold-framed, green-tinted aviator sunglass. Collecting seashells and tossing small rocks back into the ocean as it crests up along the shore, and back, as a slight breeze kicks up, blowing his hair.

Orange fringes flow with the wind, with thirteen white and red stripes on each small flag, and a blue field in the upper corner, with an image of the Milky Way Galaxy. The flags sit atop a brown Humvee that is racing down the blacktop onto the beach, dark-tinted windows surround the vehicle as it comes to a quick stop, a few meters from Bowers and the picnic goers.

The others on the beach near him turn as the Humvee stops; two men in brown and blue Marine uniforms exit the vehicle, a blonde male twenty-something Lance Corporal exits the driver's side, a single chevron pointing up and two-crossed rifles beneath on each sleeve closes the door and waits. The other man, a large African American, the rank of Sergeant Major, with three chevrons pointing up and four curving under, with a single star in the center, exits the passenger side. In his forties, with slightly gray hair mixed among his black, quickly walks up to Bowers, and stands at attention, "Commander Bowers, Sir?" he said with authority.

Bowers without missing a beat continues skipping rocks into the ocean and facing away from him, "Yes, I know a Commander Bowers, he lives about thirty kilometers north of here, Sergeant. You might have to yell a bit louder, he is deaf and in his late seventies," cupping his ear, as if deaf, still not looking at the Sergeant.

"Commander Daniel Bowers, Sir?" he repeats with more authority, "Commander Wainwright is waiting, Sir."

Bowers turned slowly, facing the Sergeant Major, and looking past him, and saw a tall lengthy blonde standing behind the passenger's side back door of the Humvee, which the Lance Corporal had opened for her. "Sergeant. . . ," he started, watching Commander Wainwright stroll down the beach toward him. The Sergeant remained at attention. She was wearing a white short-sleeved blouse and long blue slacks, with three gold stripes on both shoulder epaulets, removed her cap, white with a black brim, with gold oak leaves, and handed it to the Sergeant, who took it and returned to the Humvee, quickly.

Bowers watched as her hair fell from under her cap, and laid down along her shoulders, with a big smile on his face, as if seeing an old friend for the first time in many years. Jessica Wainwright, like Bowers, was in her early thirties, a third-generation officer, and she was an old and dear friend. They were almost married once, "I don't think that is regulation, Ma'am?" as he removed his sunglasses, with a little bit of anger in her eyes, she does not like being called Ma'am, and he knew it.

"Daniel, my sweet Daniel, how long has it been?" Commander Jessica Wainwright asked, "I do hope you enjoyed your vacation?"

"I'm retired! And he *cannot* make me come back!" Bowers yelled as he turned away and headed down the beach away from the clay wall.

"He says it's right up your alley, Dan, Dan!" she yelled back, running after him.

Still walking, waving his hand to say goodbye, "I am done!"

"They found it. . . they found it, Dan! The Goldilocks Planet, right where you said it would be."

Bowers turned back slowly, shaking his head, not wishing to go through this again, and not with him.

Bowers sat patiently on a white couch outside the office of Rear Admiral Fitzsimmons, wearing his dress uniform, blue slacks, white short-sleeved dress shirt, and blue tie, with three gold stripes along his epaulets. His cap, white with black brim, and gold oak leaves, sat next to him.

A young third-class seaman sat typing at her desk off to the right, white dress shirt, white skirt, with three black angled stripes on one sleeve, with two cross quail feathers. They both can see two people walking around in the adjacent room through the white foggy opaque window and having an intense argument, but can only hear muffled voices, and each could tell the Admiral was not happy. The smaller one of the two shifted toward the door and opened it.

Commander Wainwright stepped out of the room and looked at Bowers, smiling; he grabbed up his cap and entered.

Rear Admiral Charles Elliot Fitzsimmons III sat behind a large marble-colored wooden desk with an oversized expensive Cuban cigar in his left hand, two gold stars on his shoulder epaulets, and wearing a long-sleeved white dress shirt, and slacks. A large-sized man, bald, with an oversized bushy walrus mustache, he had been in the service for over forty years and was very old-school, especially when it came to discipline, and could not stand science types, like Bowers, or even women in the corps.

Two large flags rested behind his desk, a blue one on his left, the globe of the world's oceans with the continents, an ancient rigger ship of the eighteenth century on top, and a three-pronged triton cutting through it. The Earth flag, like the ones on the Humvee, but several times larger on his right. On the wall was an oversized map of the world, looking down from the North Pole toward the equator, he was looking over files and not happy with Bowers, and did not look up as he entered.

It was Bowers's service record, and he was disgusted with it. Bowers stood facing the Admiral at attention. Commander Wainwright stood off to the side, after closing the door, both waited, and she was still wearing the outfit from the beach.

Clearing her throat, "Sir, Commander Bowers."

The Admiral looked up to his left toward the young Commander, but not looking right at her, but more through her, begrudgingly answering her with a nod, and a slight guttural noise of disdain. Then looked quickly at Bowers, and waved his hand with the cigar, Bowers relaxed some, and the Admiral stood, crossing around his desk abruptly in front of Commander Wainwright as if she were not even standing there.

Jessica Wainwright stepped back a bit, and he walked up to Bowers, looked him over, planted his cigar in his mouth, puffing a couple of times, scanning him up and down, "Bowers is it?" Bowers's eyes watered, "I knew your Father at Annapolis. Was a bastard then, what about you?" Holding his service record up in his right hand.

Bowers coughed, "He passed three years ago, Sir."

"Damn shame. Damn, damn shame," he said, returning and crossing back to his desk, and sat, "Was a good man and a genius with computers."

"Thank you, Sir."

"Sit, Son," as he waved his hand with the cigar at the couch behind him. Jessica Wainwright sat in a chair behind her against the wall,

Bowers placed his cap next to him, glanced over at Jessica Wainwright, gave her a look of friendship, and smiled.

"Now, I do hope you enjoyed your *vacation*, Commander?" the Admiral asked.

"I was retired, Sir," Bowers advised him, but the Admiral just half glanced up and grabbed another folder from the left corner of his desk. Puffs a few more times on his cigar and places it in the ashtray, a small star-shaped glass dish with seven indentions, two larger than the rest, to hold his cigars and it sits in the center of his desk across from him. He opened the folder, looked over the first page, closed it, and passed it to Bowers, who stood, and took it. Opened it, reading it, "You can read it on the shuttle, up to the Clinton," he said gruffly and waved, dismissing them both.

Bowers and Jessica Wainwright walked down a long corridor, "Still an old bastard, isn't he? My Dad hated him."

"That is your superior officer, Commander," Jessica Wainwright explained.

He stopped abruptly, and turned back toward her, "I was enjoying my retirement, and you had to come along and screw it up."

"I was just following orders."

"Be careful, Commander, I was just following orders," mocking her, "following orders, history is full of dead men that just followed orders, and you just sat there like a bump on a log."

Jessica Wainwright gasped, "Yes, I know he despises women in uniform, but you didn't have to encourage him by just sitting there," Bowers laughed and then she laughed, "God, I have missed you, Danny," She hugged him, and smiled.

Bowers sat on a wooden bench near them and opened the file, she tried to read over his shoulder, as she sat down next to him, "So, what they got you into now, and what is a Goldilocks Planet?" Jessica Wainwright asked, still looking over his shoulder, trying to read.

He glanced over the first page, rolled it up, and over to the second, "An Earth-type planet, just far enough from the Sun that it is not too hot, and not too far from it that it's not too cold, they believe it may be acceptable for habitation," he concluded, as he skimmed the rest of the file.

"That's a good thing, right?"

He paused looking off into the distance, "If he is not involved."

The H. R. Clinton, Earth's primary space station and one of three stations orbiting Earth hangs majestically over the North American continent, two connected elongated cylinders, with three-piece smaller cylinder structures branching off, and five more separate elongated circular branching off from them, three intertwining circles, still in construction. A small six-man shuttlecraft slowly glided up from the Earth's surface and docked with one of the outer legs, nearest the Earth.

Many dark grainy ash clouds cover over sixty percent of the atmosphere and oceans since humanity has overused its resources. Mankind has neglected and destroyed its blue-green jewel for profit and greed as if profit outweighed one's survival.

The hatch slowly rose, Commander Bowers, in a brown flight suit, disembarked, seeing Rear Admiral Martinez.

Rear Admiral Ferdinand Miguel Martinez, a Hispanic light-skinned man in his late fifties, balding, and wearing a black jumpsuit with two gold stars enclosed in a thick gold square around each of his epaulets.

"Dan, old boy, it's good to see you," Martinez offered his hand, the man he wished never to see or work with again, slowly took his hand, but only shook it once and then pulled back quickly.

"Yes, Admiral."

"I hope your vacation was good at home in Texas."

"Yes, it was good to see my family again."

Martinez motioned, showing Bowers to the conference room. They entered the large room with no doors from the corridor and he saw three others waiting.

Admiral Tatsumi Nagoya, a Japanese woman in her early sixties, with graying hair pulled back, wearing a black uniform like Martinez, with four gold stars encircled in a thick gold square. She was sitting at the far end of a long conference table facing them. Two other men stood near a coffee cart, across from the entrance by a large window, which was looking down over Earth, as it was coming up on Europe to begin their day.

Senator Orrin Cooper, a young-looking man in his late forties, with thinning brown hair, and wearing a dark blue suit, with a very thin stiff collar and thin lapels, Bowers did not know him, but he could tell, the man did not wish to be there.

The other man, Professor Dmitri Ranko, an Astrophysicist from Russia, and a former Professor of Bowers's, in his late fifties, a red blotch above his right eye, among his thinning black hair, and wearing an older-style gray suit of one or two hundred years ago, and if he had slept in it. Black-framed glasses, and is sipping coffee, as Bowers and Martinez join them.

"Daniel, what has it been, five years?" Ranko yelled across the room in a friendly way, in his strong broken English, Russian accent, and then picked up Bowers in a strong bear hug.

"Eight years, your daughter's bat mitzvah," Bowers replied trying to catch his breath.

"Gentlemen?" Admiral Nagoya cuts them off, "Can we get down to business, please?" Admiral Martinez, Senator Cooper, and Bowers sat down at the far end of the table from Nagoya, "Professor Ranko, please start?"

Ranko walked to the screen behind Nagoya. "Gentlemen, and lady." He started the screen behind her, showing a Galaxy view of our system and the Sun, and it was titled *the Sol System*. "About ten years ago, when you were at the academy, you gave evidence to a planetary system that could sustain life in Galaxy M133----About two million light-years from us in the *Milky Way* Galaxy, and the *Andromeda* Galaxy, which is two and a half million light-years." He swiped his hand, and a new side appeared, showing the *Milky Way Galaxy* near the bottom, the *Andromeda Galaxy* near the top, and M133 a little below *Andromeda*. "A new single Sun star system we recently found, ten years ago, M133 which we now call *the Triton System. The Triton System* is nearly exactly like our own, with nine planets revolving around its Sun. The system has two Earth-like planets, twin sisters if you will, comparable in size to Earth and Mars. We have named them *Gamma I* and *Gamma II*. The system also has two gas giants, like Jupiter and Saturn without her rings. Here is a closer view of *Gamma II*, from just five years ago. As you can see from the probe readings, both worlds are complete deserts. Rocky barren world as Mars was back in the twenty-first century before we started terra farming and colonizing," he paused, "Ten years ago when we found this system, it was like Earth, with oceans, and teeming with vegetation and animal life. The world you told us was out there, Daniel."

"Stay on topic, please, Professor," Nagoya cut him off.

Ranko swiped his hand across the screen, and the image changed to an aerial view closer to the surface. Bowers slowly stood and walked up to the screen, followed by Admiral Martinez.

"I thought that would get your attention, Commander," Nagoya added.

Bowers studied the screen and turned toward Ranko. "A Pyramid?"

"Yes, from what we can tell. It sits in the northern hemisphere, eighty kilometers north of the equator," Ranko answered.

"Gentlemen, Gentlemen, I am a poor farm boy from a small town in Wisconsin. What's a Pyramid?" Senator Cooper asked.

"A stone structure like the Ancient Pyramids of Egypt, but this looks older, maybe as early as the Mesopotamians," Bowers explained, "You believe this planet may have been habitable at one time?"

"Yes, there must have been major clear-cutting, as Earth did in South America, back in the twentieth and twenty-first centuries, revealing the Pyramid," Ranko explained.

"That is why we called you back early, Commander," Cooper said.

"Since you are one of the leading Planetary Environmental Scientists and with your knowledge and experience in Archaeology, we would like you to finish your research. We need you and a team to go to *Gamma II* and learn all you can about the Pyramid, and find out why the planet is dead," Martinez explained.

"We are planning on terra farming the planet to help relieve the environmental issues still facing Earth and her population, and that of

Mars. With this new information, and it now being a desert, we need answers," Senator Cooper added.

Bowers looked hard at Martinez, questioning it all, then back at Ranko, "So you're telling me, that about ten years ago, there was vegetation on this world. . . Life, and now none, in just five years, it's dead?"

Ranko nodded looked at Nagoya, and then back at Bowers.

Cooper stood up slowly buttoned his jacket, putting on his best political face, and slowly placed a hand on Bowers's shoulder, "You see, Son. We have a good opportunity to finally leave our end of the Galaxy and move out truly among the stars." Bowers stood listening to all this but still looking at Martinez and knowing that this old dog was up to his old tricks again.

Martinez walked him over to the window, "Dan, we have to be sure, we have to be careful. If this gets out, there will be mass panic."

Confirming his thoughts and knowing Senator Cooper and Admiral Martinez were up to no good. His Father was never a fan of politicians, but what could he do? He needed more information.

"There is a time factor, Commander," Nagoya said.

And there it was! Bowers now knew he was not getting the whole story, and with her statement, the other shoe was dropping, which never did when it came to Admiral Martinez.

Bowers looked out the window at the planet and then turned back to Ranko again. Ranko swiped his hand over the screen again, and the solar system came back up, but this time just an area between the Sun and the twin worlds, "Each world has a six-teen-hour day cycle like Earth's twenty-four, and a four-hundred-fifty-day rotation around its Sun, like our three hundred and sixty-five days. For two hundred days, when it is the farthest from *Triton*, it has an oxygen atmosphere, but the remaining days, the atmosphere gains high levels of carbon dioxide, and becomes seventy atmospheres thicker, very much like Venus, and all this happens inside of forty-eight hours."

Bowers studied the screen. *In forty-eight hours, could never happen,* he told himself.

"That is another task you will need to explore," Nagoya advised.

Bowers rubbed his face as if all of this were a dream and all he wanted was to wake up.

Bowers sat in a small set of quarters on the space station, he did not like this line of bull Martinez was feeding him. He had left because of this man's personal agendas, and his use of the military, and now he was being brought right back into it.

A small room, very spartan, and not even one window, small for only one person, with only a bed and a table, a computer with a flat keyboard, and a vid screen above it. An old episode of *I Love Lucy,* which was playing from the nineteen sixties was played on the vid, "You have so 'spline to do Lucy."

He had files tossed over the bed as well as on the table, and a small black valor ring box sat next to the wall. He was looking through one file at the table, and quickly pushed his chair over to the bed, shuffled through the mess, and found a different file. He laid the two files next to each other and started to realize what Martinez was up to; he wanted this world, as a staging point, a military staging point for *Andromeda!*

It was not the natural resources of the planet or the terra farming as they told him, but because of its location to *Andromeda,* what did Martinez want with *Andromeda?*

I got you this time, you old bastard. He unfolded a satellite map from another folder, circled the area around the surface where the Pyramid was, and tossed the red pen on the bed.

The door chimed. He quickly pushed the folders into one pile and cleaned up the table and bed, and then picked up the ring case, and looked at the ring, a cushion cut in a square diamond in a gold band. The door chimed again. He closed it fast and shoved it in his left leg pocket, "Enter."

The door slid open. It was Jessica Wainwright, also in a brown flight suit, she entered holding two long-stemmed glasses and a bottle of champagne, "Thought we could celebrate your return to service, properly," smiled and swung both in her hands.

"Hey, Jessie."

She hugged him, still holding the glasses, and kissed him passionately, "Thought I'd give you a real welcome back, Danny."

"Yes, you were the one thing I did miss from this place," he pulled her closer and leaned her back some on the table, she dropped the glasses onto the floor, shattering, and let the bottle go, it rolled across the table.

"Commander Bowers, please report to docking bay five, Commander Bowers, docking bay five," A female's voice was heard over the PA system. Bumping his head on a shelf above the bed, scrambling out, in just his black boxers and black socks, quickly putting his flight suit back on.

"Hurry back, Danny," Jessica Wainwright said sitting up, pulling the sheet up, and covering her breasts, tucking the covers under her arms, he kissed her.

"Commander Bowers, docking bay five," Jessica Wainwright repeated, smiling at him as he ran out.

"Daniel!" Remy Mabuto calls out, as he steps out of the elevator, Bowers is running down the corridor, fixing his collar and cuffs. Doctor Remy Mabuto is a medical Doctor, an old instructor of environmental science, and medical knowledge, and an old family friend. He was wearing white surgical scrubs, and pulling off his cap. Bowers waved, glad to see him, someone he knew and someone he could trust.

They hug, "Good to see you, Remy, it's been a while."

"I am glad to see you too, Daniel, sorry I missed your Dad's funeral."

"So, I take it, they roped you into this too?"

"Someone had to look after you," Mabuto answered jokingly.

The elevator opened again, and a young Native American woman, of Cheyenne descent, mid-thirties, with the rank of Captain, nearly crashed into them, wearing a white jumpsuit, and stopped quickly, not realizing both men were there, "Gentlemen, we are about to get underway. I do hope you *both* are ready?"

Bowers looked her over and saw her name stitched on her jumpsuit: White, "Yes, Ma'am, my gear is in docking bay five, I am on my way to now, to make any last checks."

"Good," she answered and walked off past them.

"I take it this is just a normal Martinez recon mission?" Mabuto asked.

Bowers glanced around slowly to see if anyone was listening or nearby, especially Martinez, "Yes. . . and no."

Mabuto knew from that simple statement, and having been on other missions with Martinez, there would be trouble, but Bowers's answer gave it away. Bowers was not in the dark this time, not completely. Bowers had something up *his* sleeve, and maybe this time he would be able to stop Martinez before the trouble ever got started.

* * *

Gamma II 2263

Bowers sat in his quarters on a science research ship, sailing along, leaving our known galaxy. *The Albert Arnold Gore Jr.*, Earth's top-of-the-line science and research vessel, and on its way to *the Triton System.* They were a few days out. *The Gore* was one of only a few ships installed with the new quantum point-to-point drive system, able to fold space and cut the travel time by a third, between systems. A renowned physicist back in the late twenty-second century was able to fold space and time with a quantum-gravity drive. It folded space and time to shift a point in space near you. Forcing the Gravity of a Distant Star to pull the ship and slingshot it across the stars.

In the past, it took centuries or longer for sleeper-type ships to reach a neighboring galaxy, but now only a few months to reach their destinations and his of *Gamma II.* A flat elongated disk with a triangular point on one end about twenty kilometers wide, with three small drive pods like on shuttles, on each end, and one in the middle. One drive pod was situated on top and two underneath a raised section near the front for the bridge, and a protruding section near the rear, for the shuttle bay entrance.

Like his quarters on the station, this one was also small, with a console, two bunks pushed into the wall, and a locker near the door, but this time a small oval window so he could see the stars racing by. Bowers was still reading over files he had with him from *the Clinton*, as he lay on the lower bunk.

"Commander Bowers to the bridge," Captain White's voice came over the COM. He did not hear her at first and kept reading. A few seconds pass, "Commander Bowers to the bridge!"

"On my way," as he tossed the file back on the bunk, and headed out, but first placed the ring box in the locker near the door.

He entered the bridge from the elevator behind the Captain's chair, which was down a small, inclined ramp. Four stations on each side arcing around in a circle only broken by the large vid screen or the elevator, an oversized high-back chair for the Captain, who could swivel around, seeing all the stations as needed. There was a large single console in front of the Captain's chair, a young African American in her thirties was working inside it. Bowers could tell from her yellow jumpsuit; she was an Engineer and a Lieutenant from her two gold stripes.

White sat in the center chair, with two larger men in black jumpsuits standing on either side of the elevator, "We've arrived at *Gamma II*, Commander."

Doctor Mabuto entered the bridge, "The environmental equipment you asked for is ready, Dan."

"Thanks, Remy." Bowers nodded slightly toward White. White returned the nod, and Bowers reentered the elevator and left.

Entering the cargo bay, Bowers saw a large shuttle, about ten meters long and five meters tall, set to launch. There were also three small one-man fighters off to his right along the far bulkhead, with crews adding fuel to one tank, and plasma into another for weapons. He understood the fighters. This was a new place and dangerous, but this was a military-scientific mission. *A true oxymoron.* The fighters were small, about four meters front to back, three meters side to side, and a little over a meter across the cockpit, gray in color, with a glass canopy, no markings, each resting on three wheels, two in the back under the wings, and one under the nose. *We never know what is out here, and Martinez is always in an overkill mode,* Bowers thought.

"Commander, we are ready," Lieutenant Commander Sonja Appleton stated from behind him. She was the one he heard over the PA system back on *the Clinton.*

"All righty then," He motioned for her to enter first. The alarm rang out. Crew members working in the cargo bay and on the fighters grabbed up their tools and kits, exited the bay through two large metal doors on either side, and closed and sealed them tight. Red lights flooded the bay, a loud hissing noise began as the air was removed and equalized for the vacuum of space.

The large bay door opened in the center, the top panel rising, the other half lowering, horizontally. The shuttle lifted off slowly and glided out of the cargo bay and down toward the planet.

The shuttle flew over the planet, the desolate and dead world, glided over mountains and plateaus, and then circled the Pyramid a couple of times. The huge monolithic Pyramid stood majestically on the plateau, even taller than any Pyramid on Earth. The shuttle landed about a half kilometer away. Bowers stepped out first and then was joined by Appleton, and finally, two technicians in yellow and each carried vid screen, "Damn, it's hot!" one male technician said.

"Must be forty Celsius," the female technician replied.

Bowers and Appleton headed out toward the structure, both wearing white backpacks and heading north by northwest.

The Pyramid was massive, and over six kilometers high, twenty-two times higher than the Pyramid at Giza back on Earth, and three hundred meters in length. It reminded Bowers of a Pyramid, but three times larger than one he had seen in the Middle East, near the Euphrates River, in Sippar, when he was a child, on an Archaeology dig with his Mother, who was a leading Archeologist of her time. The stone looked smooth, with no weathering or tool damage that he could see, "It's huge," Appleton yelled.

The entrance was large, over thirty meters high, and cut out of stone, it looked more like a cave's entrance, and above the entrance stood a stone Ram's head, perfectly carved over three meters tall. Bowers also noticed no writing or pictographic art anywhere on the structure.

Bowers took off his pack, pulled out a screen, and started scanning the Pyramid slowly around the entrance. Appleton saw the puzzlement on his face, "Find something, Sir?"

"It is registering a force field around the Pyramid, forty watts, about a light bulb, strange?" He tapped the screen a few times, and ran it over the force field, putting his hand up and jerking back with some shock. Bowers again ran his screen up and down over the entrance.

This time the shield was gone, and he could see inside, "I see a network of corridors and chambers, leading down to a central chamber. . . and a larger chamber, and one near the bottom that my scanner still cannot read."

He turned to face Appleton, walked past her a bit, "Sonja. . ."

The ground began to shake, and he grabbed her, pulling her away from the Pyramid. Sand kicked up as a fierce wind started, like a tornado, like the ones back home on Earth, they found they were unable to keep their footing, and were tossed a few feet from the Pyramid. The ground shook again in all directions, forcing them back down.

Bowers had been in quakes before, on Earth and Mars, but this was no quake. Then it came to him this was no quake, the only thing it could be, was something was launching.

When he was a child, he had watched rockets blast off from the Capes in Florida and Hawaii. His Father would take him, his Mother, and his three Sisters on family outings, as his Father would call them, to see those massive machines exploding and flying off to parts unknown or the space stations or the moon. This time he was at ground zero, and not a safe distance across a bay, frozen at the sight of this massive monolithic structure, which was rising from the ground, nearly ten meters away. His mind told himself this could not be real; it had to be a dream and a very exhilarating dream.

His heart started racing, the massive machine ascending into the sky, with no sound of an engine roar. All they heard was the sandstorm, with sand blowing everywhere so much that they could not see.

The ship stopped dead, about twenty meters above them as did the storm, sand falling back onto the floor of the canyon, as the monolithic structure hung there as the top layer of sand trailed off, like a waterfall on each of its three sides.

The craft was dull gray in color, with some red tint from oxidation in the desert, and triangular shaped, spanning over a hundred kilometers in height and width, it was massive. Indented upward, causing the ship to be higher in the middle and on top, than the underside. Bowers could not see any seams along its edges, no tool marks, it was as if chiseled out of one piece of marble. He saw no engine turbines or any exhaust ports on the three sides.

It began to slowly turn, slowly spinning, building up speed, faster, and restarting the great sandstorm, and then shot straight up at an astronomical speed, blasting the plateau in all directions.

Bowers and Appleton were thrown back and down on the ground again. The dust settled around them, and where the ship had risen was a huge gaping hole, a crater the size of the ship, directly in front of the Pyramid that was now behind them.

He helped Appleton to her feet, "Let's get out of here!" Looking around, he quickly calculated the way back to the shuttle and pointed to his right, "This way." They both took off in a flash, running too fast, they tripped a few times, before returning to the shuttle and seeing only one technician at first. He was haphazardly cleaning up the equipment, holding on to half of a satellite dish, with the wind still blowing some. It was about fifty centimeters across and torn in half. The second technician returned with the remaining half. There were metal equipment cases and tools tossed around, and a makeshift tent torn to pieces, "What happened, Sir?" she asked joining them.

"Leave it all, we're taking off," Bowers ordered.

Once the others were safely on board, Bowers took one last look around and told himself this was not over, he would be back.

The shuttle hatch closed behind him, the engines fired off and the little craft slowly lifted off the desert floor.

Gaining altitude, and ascending into the darkness of space, all four of them in the front compartment were able to see the monolithic structure anew, which hovered above the planet. They could see its shape fully now, black as midnight with white sections on each end and a thin red line circling in-between each section of its three corners, *the Gore* was just an insect compared to it.

Appleton maneuvered the shuttle closer to *the Gore*. Its bay doors were already open. She landed it gently on the deck. White was waiting in a room on the upper level, waiting for the bay to re-pressurize. The large outer bay door closed slowly; the high-pitched whistling sound was heard again as the air returned. White ran out and slid down a ladder connected to an upper walkway, "What happened? We detected seismic activity and a storm in the area near the Pyramid."

"It was not a quake," Bowers yelled, taking the screen that White was holding, "A ship launched from the planet."

He looked over the screen, the exterior shot of the ship showed the Ancient ship in space. Alarms sounded again; they looked up at the red lights. And then back down at the screen and saw small objects exiting the ship.

Bowers swiped two fingers together over the screen, zooming in, seeing hundreds of smaller crescent-shaped ships exiting from under the massive Mother ship. Bowers tossed the screen back to White, she almost dropped it, and he ran across the bay into one of the three fighters.

White, Appleton, and the two technicians moved quickly to one of the large metal doors across the bay on the far side of the shuttle, followed by two bay technicians sealing the door shut. Two other pilots climb into the remaining fighters, already with helmets on and blast shields down. Bowers moved up the ladder to his fighter. Two other ground crew technicians help the pilots. Well, another technician handed Bowers his helmet, pulled down on the strap over his left shoulder and secured him into his chair, and tapped on his helmet.

Bowers gave a thumbs-up. The technician climbed down and rolled the ladder back as the canopy closed.

The remaining deckhands ran for the door on the opposite side of the fighters, shutting it tight. The whistling sound started again. The large cargo bay door slowly opened, and with a blast of his engine, Bowers launched, followed by the other two fighters.

Bowers and the other two fighters engage the enemy, with red lights firing out of their gun turrets, and green lights firing from the crescent-shaped ships. Bowers did a loop to loop and squared his ship up, lined up on two crescent ships, fired, and blasted one to pieces. He lost sight of the other ship in the explosion, and he nearly collided with one of his own fighters. The other fighter shot, and blasted the second one, and then swung his ship back into line with Bowers, and the other fighter.

Over the COM, "Fire, Commander!"

"Admiral Martinez?"

"I order you to fire and destroy that ship, now!"

He could not believe his ears. The Admiral wanted him to destroy the Alien ship rising from the planet, when in the past the Admiral had always wanted any new technology for himself, and he could never bring himself to kill, without just cause, and not even then, especially a new life-form, new technology. And as a scientist, he knew this was something worth studying, something new to learn. He could not bring himself to destroy it.

"I said, fire Commander! Or I will order your destruction!"

The Admiral had given him no choice. He could see the massive Alien ship now coming into view, and it was huge, spanning over a hundred kilometers in height and width, motionless and just hovering there above him in space. He tapped a few buttons on a panel to his right. Slowly his small fighter maneuvered up and above the massive Alien ship to gain a better angle of sight. From this better angle, above the massive Alien ship, he could see it completely, with all its battle damage and scarring, realizing the Alien ship was Ancient. His sensor panel lit up like a Christmas tree. An alarm sounded, then every panel in his fighter started flashing, and then a bright light illuminated and enveloped him, and then his ship, blinding his field of vision.

Bowers's ship was out of control, rolling, tumbling, head over tail, and falling toward the planet below, "Mayday, Mayday, *Gore*, can you read me? My fighter is out of control, Mayday, Mayday." But just static over the COM. He tried to stop the roll, but it was too hard, and he blacked out.

Bowers finally regained control of his fighter, but it was too late. His ship crashed into the planet. His glass canopy blasted up and back. The remaining parts of his fighter were in pieces, scattered all over the plateau, and most of it embedded in the desert floor. Bowers had a cut on his forehead, he climbed out slowly, tripped, and tumbled down on the ground, passing out again.

CHAPTER THREE

FOXES AMONG THE SHEEP

"AFTER THE EM PULSE, *the Gore's* sensors registered one other ship and we brought it aboard, it was Admiral Martinez. He would not let us check him out but had a few bruises and slight oxygen deprivation. He stayed with White, as far as I remember, and we could not detect your fighter, Dan," Mabuto explained as the others sat on the far side of the large conference table. Bowers sat at the other end, alone, just the large table and eight chairs, a large window off to his right, and the door behind him, "We learned later, like Martinez, we all had been unconscious for five hours."

Walker-Swanson found Mabuto's story hard to believe, as she did Bowers's, and still does not trust him, "And all you remember was walking through the desert at night?"

"Yes. . . and remembering more now, I must have gotten up and started walking, how I lost ten years is still a mystery to me," Bowers explained. Walker-Swanson rolled her eyes in utter disbelief.

"After we brought Martinez's ship onboard *the Gore,* there were no other ships in the quadrant," Mabuto continued, "White ordered sensor sweeps, and had teams search for you for days, but no luck, you were nowhere, and no debris of your fighter could be found, then we were recalled. Once back on Earth, Martinez logged your death, and after reading White's, Appleton's, and my reports, classifying them, as well as the mission and planets."

Bowers just sat there, realizing Martinez needed him dead, and knowing why, *Andromeda*. Macpherson broke the silence first, "A year ago, they were looking to start this station up again and continue *your* mission, I jumped at it, because some in the Admiralty and I knew, if you were alive, you'd be here." Bowers leaned forward, starting to speak, but she cut him off again, and continued, "It has been quiet for the last six months, we have gone to the Pyramid twice, once even clean up the mess, you had left behind, but the field you reported was active. again. Mitchell, you, and Walker-Swanson continue with the code Chief Adams uploaded. Remy, how are Hitchcock and Adams doing?"

"Both are still unconscious and should awake shortly. Hitchcock's injuries are minor, just a sprained arm and a few bruises, and Chief Adams's swelling has reduced."

Walker-Swanson watched Bowers closely, as she and Mitchell left, leaving Mabuto, Macpherson, Swanson, and Bowers, "Were you able to gain access to the Pyramid last time?" Macpherson asked.

"No, while exploring the entrance, the shield dropped, and the ship launched, I must have woken something up, or the ship was already planning on launching due to *the Gore* in orbit," Bowers answered.

"Once Hitchcock's and Adams's conditions improve, we can finish *your* original mission," Macpherson said.

"Do you really believe this hogwash he is trying to sell us?" Walker-Swanson asked.

"The Doctor has confirmed his identity, he is Bowers, and we know something happened at the Pyramid, which is not far from Waterman Crater, and we both have felt the quakes on the far side of the planet," Mitchell explained, "The two incidents are tied together, and we should look into it, right?"

"I don't know anymore, Thomas, I do know, I don't trust him," she said as they entered Engineering.

"Doctor, my sensors are detecting that Commander Hitchcock is waking, now," *Gamma* reported.

They hurried to the medical bay. Hitchcock was sitting up now as the four entered, taking his sling off, "What the bloody hell happened to me?" Hitchcock asked with a strong British Accent, "And who the hell are you?" upon seeing Bowers.

"This is Commander Daniel Bowers," Macpherson answered.

Hitchcock gave her a look as if she was crazy, "Bowers, he's been dead for over ten years."

"Missing in Action, presumed dead, and only because nobody had found his body after three years," the Doctor said.

"I've missed a lot," Hitchcock said.

"We crashed due to the magnetic storm, caused by a solar flare, knocking you against one of the bulkheads, and unconscious, and the *Gamma* station, which we believe, also happened ten years ago, did not kill Bowers but brought him to this point in time," Macpherson summarized.

"And *my* equipment?" Hitchcock asked impatiently.

"Mitchell has looked it over. . . " Macpherson answered.

Hitchcock cut her off degradingly, "I do hope that kid *knows* what he is doing," as he jumped off the bed and walked out at a brisk pace.

Doctor Mabuto was not happy, he wanted to check him out fully.

"What an ass," Bowers said.

Swanson moved to the console. Macpherson and Mabuto looked at each other, rolling their eyes and smiling, as if to agree with him, but neither of them would say it out loud.

Bowers turned to his left and faced Chief Adams, "So, how's the Chief?"

Mabuto turned around facing Chief Adams, "He should be awake by morning. His swelling has reduced, and his nervous system is functioning normally."

Bowers turned to the Captain, "You think I could get any information out of Swanson about what happened before the EM pulse?" He asked looking over at Swanson, hoping she did not hear him.

Macpherson looked over at Swanson to see if she was listening, "I might. I do not think Walker-Swanson will let you go anywhere near her wife. She doesn't believe a thing you have said."

"Then I leave that to your capable hands, Captain."

"Doctor, please advise me once Chief Adams is awake," Macpherson asked.

The shuttle was now back in the cargo bay and Mitchell was checking it over with a screen in his right hand and a long glass rod similar to the one he had earlier, about fifty centimeters long. Hitchcock stopped him and took the screen. "How is my equipment, boy?"

Mitchell paused, "Sir, I have looked it over, and from what I can see, there is no damage."

"I'll look for myself," Hitchcock blurted as he entered the shuttle.

Under his breath, "Asshole," Mitchell said without looking back and walked out of the cargo bay and continued into Engineering. He sat at the center console, picked up a new screen, and laid it back down.

A tall black cloaked figure over three meters tall entered from a room behind him, it touched his shoulder and Mitchell turned. Seeing the face under the cloak, he went pale, and collapsed on the floor, in shock. The cloaked figure picked up the screen, looked it over as if it were a child's toy, dropped it, and left the way it came.

Walker-Swanson enters and climbs up the ramp to the center console, "Thomas, you still in here?" Seeing Mitchell on the floor, she checked his pulse, "Computer, inform the Doctor he is needed in Engineering!"

"Yes, Ma'am," *Gamma* replied.

She turned Mitchell over; his face was still ghostly white, and his eyes were wide open. The Doctor and Swanson entered, Swanson placed him on a stretcher, and they carried him out.

The three carry Mitchell out as the door to Engineering closes behind them, and a menacing laugh cried out.

The three enter the med bay, placing Mitchell on the farthest bed from Chief Adams. The green light scanned him, the Doctor walked over to the console, and picked up a screen, tapping a few times.

Macpherson and Bowers arrived, "What happened?" Macpherson asked.

"Ask him!" Walker-Swanson yelled lunging at Bowers.

Macpherson stopped her, "We have talked about this, Lieutenant. Either work with us or you're confined to quarters."

"I found Thomas in Engineering like this," she answered pointing at Mitchell on the bed.

The Doctor returned, "He is in shock, and from all reports he took a massive dose of electricity."

"Will he recover, Doc?" Swanson asked.

"With time and rest."

Chief Adams moaned from the far bed, rubbing his forehead, "Did anyone get dat number of dat space cruiser dat hit me?" with a hard Brooklyn accent.

"How do you feel, Chief?" Mabuto asked.

"Death warmed over."

Macpherson put her hand out toward Bowers, snapping her fingers; he opened his top pocket of his left sleeve and handed her the disk, "Do you know what this is, Chief?"

Chief Adams took it, looked it over, and after a long pause, "Nope, never seen that before."

"We found this in your neck," Bowers told him.

Adams looked at Bowers, paused, thinking, and then recognized him, "Commander Bowers?"

"Do I know you, Chief?"

"No, Sir, not personally, but I had seen your face on a few vid screens when you were negotiating for Mars during the Riots. I want to thank you for dat, we didn't think anyone was listening to us, colonists. . . But you're dead, Sir?"

"Long story, for another time," Bowers said. He offered Adams the screen he was carrying, and continued, "Do you know this subroutine?"

Looking down at the screen, "No, Sir."

"I found this in the system after I found you out cold in Engineering," Bowers explained.

"I was out cold because that Lesbian bitch knocked me out!" Adams replied, pointing at Swanson. Walker-Swanson stepped forward, ready to kill him, but Macpherson motioned again to stop her.

"Stick to the facts, Chief, and leave out the commentaries, this isn't a bar on Saturday night," Bowers ordered.

"All I remember, Sir, is I was working at my console, and she came at me with a wrench," Adams explained.

"Somehow this disk," Bowers explained taking the disk back from Macpherson, "took over your mind, as you were trying to destroy the station with this subroutine, Swanson found you, tried to stop you, you both struggled, and you knocked her out, put her in the moon pool, and when you returned, the pulse hit, and you passed out, hitting the console as you fell."

"Pulse?" Adams asked with confusion.

"An electromagnetic pulse from the Sun," Bowers answered. Adams looked at him, very confused, "This is resistance tech, Chief!"

"I have no idea, Sir, what you're talking about."

"Can he return to work, Doc?" Macpherson asked.

"He should be locked up, Ma'am!" Swanson yelled.

"I agree with you, Ensign, but since Mitchell is out cold, we need someone to work on the station and repair the shuttle," Macpherson reminded her, "With Mr. Mitchell out cold, Chief, I need you to get the station up and running, and the other shuttle ready."

"Yeah," sarcastically with a funny two-finger salute, jumps off the bed and leaves.

Macpherson hits the bed with her fist, "That bigoted bast---- "

"Let it go, Bekka, we have other things to worry about right now," Bowers said, with concern.

"Yes,"

Hitchcock was now working in the shuttle's front compartment, in the pilot's chair as Chief Adams joined him, "I never understood why Earth Alliance gave her the Command and not you!"

"What did the bitch do now, Earl?"

"Nothing, she's a *woman*," he said, emphasizing the word woman, hard.

"I hear ya,"

Chief Adams sat down in the command chair and started tapping buttons, "What did dat boy do now? My shuttle is a fucking mess!"

"I was out cold, I don't know. The shuttle rocketed hard during the storm. That's all I remember," Hitchcock answered, "At least my equipment was not damaged."

"Well, whatever happened, *us* men will fix it," Adams said, pointing first at Hitchcock, then back at himself with his left thumb.

"True, but why is Bowers back?" Hitchcock asked.

"Last, I knew he was dead. However, was one hell of a negotiator for the residence on Mars, then was lost over this planet ten years ago," Adams explained, "I guess the EM Pulse they are talking about happened ten years ago and had shot him through time."

Hitchcock looked at him over his small black reading glasses, as if hard to believe.

"Who knows? It's what the *woman* told me, and you know women, they don't know shit," Adams said.

"Yeah," Hitchcock replied not even listening to him, leaving and slapping Adams on his shoulder.

Chief Adams, alone in the shuttle now, leaned up and looked out the window making sure he was alone, and then pulled a small square silver radio from his lower pocket of his right leg. Turned it on, and then pulled out a small earpiece from the same pocket, placed the earpiece into the radio, and his ear, "Bravo twelve to Alpha, over----Bravo twelve to Alpha, over."

"Alpha, go, Bravo twelve, over." Martinez's voice came over the radio, "You're late checking in, over."

"EMP and Magnetic storm shut us down for a time, over."

"Did you activate the subroutine, over?"

"No, not yet, *and* we have a bigger problem, Alpha, over."

"What? Over."

"Bowers *is* alive, and here, over."

There was a long pause, then, "Fifty years before Ranko projected, over," Martinez answered.

"What are your orders, Alpha? Over."

"Learn what he knows, kill him. He will not stop my plans, or control that station, over."

Macpherson was working in Command, when Bowers came in and shifted around the center console, and faced her, "I don't know how you can work with those two idiots."

"Hitchcock is just upset because I am in Command, it was to be his, but I guess, someone was watching out for me. Adams is just a damn bigot. Can we talk about something else, please?" she said, rubbing her forehead.

"I think they're the least of our worries right now. I still don't believe Chief Adams. He lied; he knows that tech."

Macpherson swung around to leave, facing the door, and saw Calvin standing there, "You left me!" he yelled in an ancient and powerful voice, echoing as if through a wind tunnel, and then collapsed onto the floor.

"He's dead," Bowers said as he checked his pulse, and then Calvin's body faded away slowly.

"What evil did you wake up?" Macpherson asked.

"I wish, I knew, but he was the one that knocked me across the room the other day."

Many hours later Bowers was still in Command going over more data, and the time he had lost, "*Gamma*, I read here that Martinez and Ranko headed up the construction of this station, can you find any more information regarding this?"

"The only information I have in my data files since I still cannot Uplink with Earth, is that they arrived a few years after *the Gore* was recalled, with a crew, built this station, and then returned to Earth. Any other activities they had were never documented," *Gamma* summarized.

"What logs did *the Gore* have after the EM pulse?"

"Mine and the Gore's core data was erased by the pulses, not available. The system is waiting for a new Uplink to restore my data files."

"I bet Martinez erased it all," Bowers said under his breath.

"Was that a question, Bowers?"

"No, just thinking out loud, *Gamma*. The Admiral is covering something up, and not just my disappearance. Did Professor Ranko add any additional information on the planet or the Pyramid, after my disappearance?"

"Professor Ranko does state in a report, dated two years after your disappearance----that we may not be alone on this planet nor in this quadrant of space."

"And let me guess, no one believed him."

"Professor Ranko was disavowed by Earth Military, Earth Alliance, and the Russian consortium, and most of the scientific community, five years after your disappearance. The official medical record stated he developed a mental setback and depression because of his age, and he never really got over your death," *Gamma* advised.

"Between the time of the solar flare ten years ago and Martinez building this station, were there any other surveys done or scientific studies on the planet?"

"From the time of your disappearance, till two years before this station came online, Admiral Martinez had put a quarantine status on this planet. Then a year ago, the counsels of Earth and Mars felt it was time, due to the continuing environmental concerns on Earth, and this station was reactivated. Martinez protested vehemently, but he was ignored, as Vice Admiral Wainwright stated in one report, "We can easily work around the solar flares," *Gamma's* voice changed to that of Vice Admiral Andrew Jackson Wainwright.

"You've been here all night?" Macpherson asked, entering.

Bowers looked up and out the window. The Sun was rising, "Yeah, must've been," he answered as he stretched.

"Did you find any answers?"

"Found more questions, than answers. Who is your Commanding Officer, and had assigned you to this post?"

"Mars Military Commander, Admiral Andrew Jackson Wainwright.

And with that, Bowers's mind raced back to Jessica Wainwright, the Admiral's daughter, with fawned affection.

"So, you've had no contact with Admiral Martinez?"

"Other than knowing of him and only by reputation, Admiral Martinez retired six years ago, no," Macpherson answered, sitting down at the forward console.

"That would have been a vital piece of information I needed, *Gamma*."

"That was not one of your questions, Commander Bowers," *Gamma* answered, Macpherson smiled, "Admiral Martinez resigned after his protests to the counsels regarding this planet were ignored."

"What were his protests?" Bowers knew Martinez was not out of the game yet.

"Officially, he stated to the counsels and the Admiralty that the solar flares and the high levels of carbon dioxide period of this planet were both unsafe."

"And unofficially?" Macpherson asked.

"Reports and rumors floated around that he wanted it for himself. He had *the Gore* take many surface scans of both planets, *Gamma I* and *Gamma II*, and of the *Andromeda Galaxy,* and many sensor scans of the ship before it disappeared, but he never disclosed the reports," *Gamma* explained.

"Why then did he want this planet so bad. . .?" Macpherson asked.

Over the COM, Mitchell called out, "Captain, can you join me in cargo bay two?"

Entering cargo bay two, she and Bowers saw Mitchell exiting a second shuttle, *the Muir,* named after the famous naturalist John Muir of the nineteenth century. There was also a metal-framed Jeep off to one side and many crates.

"How are you, Mitchell?" Macpherson asked.

"Better, Ma'am. I found something *you* both need to see," Turning back into the shuttle, they followed, and saw Calvin lying on the deck.

"You called the Doctor?" Macpherson asked.

"Yes, he is on his way."

The Doctor scans Calvin's body with a screen and then looks up at the Captain with confusion, "He is alive?"

"How can that be? You stated he was dead at the crater," Macpherson said.

"He is alive now, but unconscious, we need to get him back to the medical bay, fast."

Bowers grabbed Calvin by his shoulders while Mitchell took him by his legs and they ran out, and Mabuto followed. Macpherson stayed behind and continued to look over the shuttle.

Doctor Mabuto, Bowers, and Mitchell enter carrying Calvin. Swanson followed them over to one of the beds.

"Complete scan, please?" Mabuto called out. The green light washes over his body.

"I thought he was dead?" Swanson asked.

"He was," Mabuto answered.

Calvin started moving, "Water?" with a soft horsed voice.

Swanson grabbed a canteen from a cabinet behind the bed. She put the opening to his lips, "Slowly, just a little bit now."

Calvin looked at Bowers, "Who are you?"

"Long story," Mabuto answered, he looked from Bowers to Calvin, "Computer, report?"

"Lieutenant Calvin is suffering from dehydration."

"Dehydration, nothing more?"

"He needs treatment or may lose his kidneys."

"What was the last thing you remember?" Swanson asked.

Calvin pauses, thinking, "Slamming face-first into the shuttle console."

"That was three days ago!" Swanson blurted out.

Mabuto shoots a stern look at her, "Is this not your date night?"

Swanson bit her lower lip, knowing she should not have said that, and ran out.

"Three days? What the. . ."

"You were dead," Mabuto cut him off.

"What, how?" Calvin started, but the shock came over him, and got agitated.

Doctor Mabuto jabbed a hypo-spray into his arm. Calvin fell back, "He will be out for a couple of hours, and hopefully better when he awakes."

"Yes, and maybe some answers," Bowers commented.

Macpherson entered with a long black cloak draped over her right arm, "I found this in the shuttle. How's Calvin?"

"He was all right until Swanson stated he was dead for three days," Mitchell replied, "so the Doc knocked him out with some hydro-cord."

"Septinal, a nerve suppressant," Doctor Mabuto corrected him, "He will be out for some time, now."

Bowers walked over to Macpherson, "What you got there?"

"Not sure, I found it stuffed into one of the lockers in the back storage," Macpherson answered.

"Hitchcock, I need your help," Adams asked, as he stepped into the conference room.

Not looking up, holding a screen with many others around him on the conference table, "Yes?"

"I know the bitch conned you out of your job, and I know how we can screw her out of it,"

Hitchcock looked up slowly, "Listening?"

"I have been in contact with Admiral Martinez, and he is not happy that Bowers has returned."

"He's not alone."

"Martinez wants me to kill Bowers, but I feel we should make it look like an accident and have Macpherson holding the bag, and then the Command here, will fall to you," Adams explained, sitting down across the table from him.

Hitchcock looked up, thinking, "May work. What you have in mind?"

"Martinez gave me a subroutine, which I added to the computer days after we arrived. It will start a terra farming program but will not work as planned and I will also need some figures from you, and then I can make it look like Macpherson entered the wrong code, and as you know, whoever is left on the planet once it starts will be dead, both of them on the planet, both dead," Adams explained, sliding a screen across the table that he was holding.

Hitchcock picked the screen up and looked it over, "Not bad, may work," Scratching his chin, "As long as we can keep him on the planet also. They will think the terra farming failed, and she will be blamed. I'll tell Earth, from a nice safe shuttle in orbit that she went mad with shock because of his return from the dead," he explained, analyzing the situation.

"They will give you the Command and this planet will be ours," Adams said.

"Mine!"

Swanson entered her quarters. The lights were dimmed, "Kathy?"

Walker-Swanson turned the bathroom light on. She was wearing a silky white teddy with a silk robe hanging off her shoulders, "Hello, lover," she strolled over toward her, meeting her near the bed, they kissed and held each other close, and fell back onto the bed. Kissing and caressing, Walker-Swanson slowly unzipped her jumpsuit, revealing her large breasts, and started kissing down her neck.

Alarms rang out, red lights started flashing, and each looked up with shock, "What the fuck, now!" Walker-Swanson yelled.

CHAPTER FOUR

MOON BASE: TRINITY

THIRTEEN YEARS AGO

"FIRE, COMMANDER!"

A small short-range shuttlecraft hovered over Gamma II, a cramped ship with only one occupant, Admiral Martinez. Six meters by four meters, oval-shaped, with a slopping large window in front, one sat behind the console that arced around the front under the window. A bright light flashed from behind the small shuttlecraft and enveloped it.

"What the fuck!" Martinez yelled. His small craft tumbled, over and over, with sparks flying everywhere and smoke filling the cockpit. He tried franticly to stabilize the ship. A blue light enveloped his small craft.

"Admiral Martinez, we've got you in our tractor beam and are bringing you in the shuttle bay," over the COM, Captain White advised.

The shuttle slowly proceeded. The blue beam continued around his shuttle and lowered it gently onto the deck. The outer doors closed, and the air returned.

Two deckhands dressed in silver fire-suppression suits, oversized silver pants, wide black boots, and oversized silver jackets with red and yellow stripes, on their backs with oversized lines crossing, in an X. Glowing, so others can see them anytime, even in the dark, with oversized silver covering for their heads, a large black square in the front for them to see and protect their faces. Both were using extinguishers on the shuttle to put out the smoke that was coming from the underside and the back of the shuttle, in case of a fire after the oxygen returned to the bay.

Admiral Martinez stumbled out, coughing, and landed face-first on the deck, wearing all-black civilian clothing, jeans, a turtleneck sweater and a jacket, and heavy work boots. A female brunette medical technician tried to place a mask over his mouth with a small canister of oxygen.

Captain White slid down the straight metal ladder from the level above, "Admiral, are you all right?"

Pushing the mask off, fighting the medical technician, who knew he needed the oxygen, she just knelt beside him, "I am fine!" He pushed her away and stood. Captain White motioned toward the technician to step back and wait. She sat on the deck, holding the canister.

"Sit rep! And where the hell is that ship?"

"The ship is gone, Sir," White advised.

"What happened?" Catching his breath.

"A solar flare from the Triton Sun, the system stated we had been out for five hours. When we came back online, we saw your ship rolling out of control," White reported.

"Bowers destroyed it?"

"No, Sir."

He looked straight through her, "He defied my orders? Where is he?" Standing up again regaining his dignity.

"No, Sir, we don't know, since the solar flare, he and the Alien ship are no longer detected on short or long-range sensors," she explained, not knowing if he did shoot or not, just didn't want to upset him anymore.

"And where is he? And that ship?"

"The Ancient ship is gone, and Bowers is Missing in Action, Sir," White answered, "The other two fighters are in pieces out there."

He took a deep breath and let it out slowly, looked down at the deck and then back up at White harshly, and walked quickly for the hatch behind his shuttle, "White, you're with me!"

Doctor Mabuto had reached the cargo bay and looked at the medical technician just sitting there, "The shit is going to hit the fan now."

Two other bay technicians looked over at him and understood what he meant by the statement, and then he helped the medical technician to her feet.

Martinez and White emerged on the bridge. They walk over to a station nearby. She tapped a few times, and he leaned down, looking over the sensor reports. The screen showed the planet and nothing else, but debris from two fighters and many of the crescent-shaped ships.

"So, there has been no communication from Bowers, and no other debris?" Martinez asked.

"None, Sir, just the other two fighter's wreckage," White answered.

"I need a private room, with a private channel, and a probe sent to these coordinates," he ordered as he tapped a few buttons. "And, Captain, no one sees the probe's reports but me, understand?" he ordered with a sharpness in his voice.

She nodded and waved to a large dark-skinned Samoan man, who was standing near the elevator, wearing a black jumpsuit with no insignia or rank, "Please show the Admiral to the briefing room and wait outside, give him any assistance he needs," The man stepped back, and the elevator opened.

The Admiral looked down at the sensor reports again, then back up at her, and stormed out. The dark-skinned Samoan man followed.

The Admiral sat at the end of the long table, typing on a keypad. The screen across the room went from black to white, and then a sharp image of Senator Cooper, "We have a problem, Orrin. We have a major problem. Bowers is missing, and there is a hole in the ground. It's as large as the size of the Grand Canyon and is next to the Pyramid. A fucking Alien ship launched," the Admiral said quickly, but choose his words carefully.

"He's dead?"

"Fuck if I know. A damn solar flare happened, and we were all out for five hours, and he and the Alien ship are gone!"

"And . . ."

"And . . ." Martinez replied, "it's a cluster-fuck!"

"I'll talk with Ranko. . . better quarantine the planet."

"Already in the works," as he tapped a few times on the keypad.

"Contact me when you're back on Mars," Cooper said.

Admiral Martinez tapped the table, the Senator faded, and the screen returned to black, "What the fuck, Dan!"

PRESENT DAY

COPPERHEAD MINE
EARTH ALLIANCE
IO 2215

The bronze plaque sat embedded into the concrete wall of the *IO* spaceport, with people hurrying about moving from location to location in the shuttle port, coming, and going to Earth, Mars, and the colonies beyond *the Sol System.*

The *IO* shuttle port was a place where if someone wanted to get away or disappear, they could, and for parts unknown, or home to Mars and Earth.

Mining for precious metals, water, and a new liquid methane fuel source, unlike fossil fuel on Earth, this methane fuel was a pure liquid, with no need for refining.

Martinez scanned the area watching all the decadence and commercialism. Space now came with a price.

Martinez was standing on an elevated ledge being lowered to the floor from the shuttle bays above, an open elevated ledge with a metal ceiling. The elevated ledge was on the east side of the spaceport.

It stopped. He stepped off. He was wearing the clothing of a miner, blue work jeans, black work boots, and a white nylon sleeveless jacket, with a grey long-sleeved T-shirt underneath. He was now also sporting a small black goatee with a splash of gray, and balding more, with only a bit of gray on the sides of his head.

He moved slowly through the crowd of people and wished not to be seen. He was carrying a small metal briefcase and pulling an oversized metal rolling case, and he then noticed two men, one with black hair and a beard, in his late forties, and the other in his late thirties, but could still pass for one right out of high school, with blonde hair. Both men were wearing the same outfit as Martinez. The bearded man was in a gray nylon jacket and the blonde man was in a blue nylon jacket, all three men looked just like all the other miners working on *IO* and *Ganymede.*

The bearded man nodded to get Martinez's attention, and looked over at two guards near the stairs, both in black jumpsuits and one with a vacuum rifle. A slim barrel rifle about half a meter long with a simple framed stock, and a small tube along the top, with liquid bullets, real bullets could cause decompression damage. If shot at or near a bulkhead near the vacuum of space, liquid bullets will cause no damage and if shot at a body, it will still hurt like hell, but stop a suspect in his tracks.

Martinez looked over where the bearded man was looking and saw the two guards. He nodded back at the blonde and dropped his larger metal case. The bearded man picked it up and walked back the way Martinez came. The blonde man waited a bit, looked around, and then followed Martinez once he knew the guards were not watching.

Martinez walked past the guards and down a set of stairs, turned right, and down another set of stairs, and into another corridor, a lower level. He sat on a metal bench.

The blonde man walked past him some and up to a makeshift newsstand, metal walls, and one large opening in the front, with stacks of magazines and newspapers. The blonde man took a newspaper from behind a metal bar, and placed a thin white card on a screen, on the ledge, next to it was a sign that read, "Back in 20 minutes," handwritten.

The paper was titled, *Colonial Press*, "Is everything in order to get me to *Gamma II*?" Martinez asked quietly. so only the blonde man could have heard him.

The man turned the page and snapped it, folding it up in half under his arm, "Yes, just waiting on final confirmation of payment," with a low voice, not to draw attention. "Head up to the Embassy tower, you're registered under Jiménez, three stories up the north tower," He dropped a small manila envelope in the trashcan between them and walked off.

Martinez watched the man leave, waited a bit longer as people continued to walk by, stood, picked up the envelope, opened it, took a small disk out and a flat white plastic card, similar to the blonde man's, and placed them inside his right jacket pocket.

Heading off the way he came, he turned right and was about to step onto the stairs to the main level again, but was stopped by the same two guards, "Admiral Martinez, please come with us," the larger of the two men requested, who had a long old scar down his left cheek.

"My name is Jiménez," Martinez stated, "and here are my papers," as he handed him the small disk. The man took it, placed the disk into a watch-like device on his left wrist, and it flashed a small three-dimensional image of the Admiral, in the same miner's clothing he had on, and it slowly rotated around, with a caption below and a male voice narrated, "Señor José Jiménez, contactor, electrical firm, Mars sector, on assignment with Copperhead Mine Corps." Martinez looked down and rolled his eyes, *so Original for these mercenaries,* he thought.

"Seems all is in order, Señor Jiménez, you looked like the man we have been looking for," the larger man said, as he handed him his disk back.

"Hope you find your man."

He reached the elevated ledge on the north end of the shuttle port and waited for it to rise and turned around. The elevated ledge rose slowly, "Embassy tower?" He scanned the room again and watched the two same guards who stopped him, questioning another man. *Idiots,* as he watched them arrest him. The man looked like him, barely, taller, and white, with blonde hair.

The elevator stopped and the doors opened onto an elegant lobby of a high-class hotel, most of the men were wearing expensive tuxedos and the women were expensive ball gowns, the rest, miner's clothing.

Decadence, he thought, as he looked around the room and crossed the lobby, to the front desk.

A young dark-haired Indian girl waited, dressed in her authentic Indian Sari dress, with a section missing around her abdomen and a jade stud with a gold chain in her belly button, "May I help you, Sir?" with a slight high-pitched Indian accent.

"I have a reservation, my name is Jiménez," he handed her the small white plastic card from his jacket pocket.

She laid the card on a small screen next to her keypad on the counter; his data appeared on the screen, "Yes, Sir. Here, you are in room 140," she replied and turned around and typed 140 into a small metal box with a number pad on the counter behind her. A plastic transparent card slowly exited from the wall above the keypad, smaller than the card he gave her, "Room 140, Sir, this hallway," pointing to his left.

"Thank you," he took the card and walked down the corridor.

Martinez sat on the edge of a small bed in his small hotel room, with an awful brown shag carpet and drapes, green bedding, and red lampshades, the room's style was seventies disco classic from the twentieth century, even having a large disco ball as the ceiling lamp. He wished people would stop trying to reinvent the past on this pathetic of a level, cleaning his old .45 pistol, *my old friend*. He loved old weapons and placed each part back into the gun precisely, slid it back on top, and finally placed the clip into the butt, sliding it back and disarming it. Placed it down on the bed next to him, on a red silk cloth, and picked up an additional clip, added bullets gently, from a box, in his briefcase on the bed behind him, to his right.

When finished, he put the filled clip in his inside left pocket, picked up the red silk cloth, and started wiping down the pistol.

A single shape chime sounded: he tossed the cloth on the bed, cocked the gun, and looked through the small eyehole within the door. Disarmed it, removed the chain, and opened the door.

Senator Cooper and the two men from earlier in the shuttle port strolled in, Cooper now with gray hair on his temples, and also in a miner's outfit, with a yellow jacket, "Is it true?" He crossed the room and sat at the small table near the drapes.

"Yes, Bowers is back, talked with my contact two days ago," as he chained the door.

"And when will you be on *Gamma II*?"

Martinez looked over at the bearded man, "Less than a week," he stated in broken English, with a strong Russian accent.

Cooper looked at Martinez, "Good," and walked back to the door, unchained it, and walked out swinging the door closed behind him.

The door did not close fully, and the blonde man stepped up and closed it.

"When do we depart?" Martinez asked.

"Zero three-thirty, *IO* standard time," the bearded man replied.

"Did you find the second squad, I asked for?"

"Yes, just need to know where we meet up."

"Here," Martinez pulled two maps from the top of his briefcase, and laid them on the table, a lunar map, "First, we will gain access to Moon Base: *Trinity* on *Gamma I's* moon for a power core. The second squad will join up with us here," pointing down on a section of the lunar map, "Then, we will travel from there to an old research station here, on *Gamma II*, sixty kilometers east of the *Gamma II station* in Schmitt's Gorge. Here," snapping his fingers and pointed down on the second map of *Gamma II*, labeled Schmitt's Gorge, "Only a few key people and I know of it," Martinez explained.

The Russian shook his head in agreement.

Cooper sat in a small vid booth, with only a chair and console, and closed the glass door slowly, he watched the room slowly; he placed his card into a slot in the wall under the vid screen. The console lit up; a small panel slid back, revealing a small number pad. He tapped out 1776, and the vid screen activated. A tall Asian man with dark slicked-back hair, sat behind a desk, in a black suit, wearing an old-style metal pin of the Earth flag on his left lapel. Sitting behind an oversized desk with three large windows behind him, the Oval Office of the President of Earth with Rear Admiral Fitzsimmons next to him. They were going over some papers. Fitzsimmons was trying to keep his oversized cigar away from the President, but not doing a good job, and the President was not pleased with the amount of smoke.

There were two flags behind him, one, the flag of the universe, and the other, the flag of the Earth President, in a blue field with thirteen stars circling around a bald eagle, holding olive branches in its right talon, and arrows in its left.

The President looked up, seeing Cooper, "Things going as planned?" Cooper heard his strong Korean accent.

Cooper looked out, to his left and right again, and then back to the vid screen, "Yes, Mr. President, Martinez is here on *IO* gaining the last of his remaining resources and manpower and will depart onto Moon Base: *Trinity* in the *Triton System*."

"Good, *Gamma II* still dark?" The President asked.

"Yes, *the Roosevelt* is sitting nearby just out of sensor range, jamming their frequencies," Cooper explained, as Fitzsimmons glanced up slightly, looking at Cooper; this was the first time he had heard of this, and was very confused.

The President nodded, "I do hope Admiral Martinez is right about this and we have nothing to worry about, even now, since Bowers has returned, the *Andromeda* mission cannot fail!"

This was the first Fitzsimmons had heard about Bowers's return, but kept his emotions in check, not showing his hand to Cooper or the President.

"Yes," Cooper answered.

"You will be back on Mars in time for the Summit?" the President asked.

"Yes," Cooper replied.

"Good," The President looked up and to his right, to someone behind his vid screen, and nodded, the vid screen went black; Cooper tapped the # key on the pad, and his card slid out some, and he looked around one last time, and left.

*   *   *

Moon Base: *Trinity* sat on *Gamma I's* moon, abandoned and unused for over six years, built as a relay station for communications between *the Sol System* and beyond for deep space probes and exploration ships moving into *the Andromeda* Galaxy. *Trinity* was the only moon either planet possessed; its rotation has always kept it on the far side of *Gamma II*. Because of this, Martinez knew it was a good place to stage his plan, so no one would see him coming. There was no atmosphere on this dead rock in space, similar to Earth's moon.

The communication station had five legs extending from the circular central hub, the same design as *Gamma II*, without the pumping station that terrestrial sites used.

Ten small specks started across the surface slowly hopping, moving into view along the open terrain of *Trinity*, all dressed in environmental suits, and all in black except three, green, blue, and white. The low gravity allowed hopping as a faster pace, inching their way to the station with the remaining black-suited one's half circling the inner group.

The outer group slowly and haphazardly approached the inner group, the blue-suit man pulled his backpack off and placed it on the lunar surface, kneeling with one knee. Pulling a small screen and two long cables out, attaching the cables to the screen at the top, and then sliding down a small panel above the number pad, with alligator clips, attach one lead onto a single metal wire inside the panel. The other, he clipped to a small black cylinder up inside along the left, stretching his fingers deep inside, and then tapped the screen, the door slid open a few centimeters.

The individual in white waved three of the larger ones near the back, they stepped up, and grabbed the door at different points, shoving the door to the far left. The remaining group entered the station as the blue-suited man unclipped the cables, collected up his screen and backpack, and shifted inside.

Once inside, the blue-suited man again placed his pack on the deck, slid the panel down on this side, clipping the two leads up inside, as he did outside, and tapped on the screen. The door closed fully; he tapped some more, and the lights started coming on from the far end of the room, a few more taps, he looked down at his screen, and tapped once again.

A loud hissing sound started as the air returned to the room and base, an old scrap of paper flew across the room as the room was re-pressurized. The blue-suited man removed the cables and placed the screen and cables on the shelf near him. He unlocked his helmet and removed it. Revealing the blonde man, Martinez met back on *IO*, "Good to go, a bit stale but workable."

In the center of the group, the man in white removed his helmet, revealing Admiral Martinez, "Good job, Mr. Smith."

The inner door of the base slid open, revealing all the men now without the environmental suits, all but four in black jumpsuits. They are now in miner's clothing, the blonde man called out from the back of the group, "By the time you get to Command, the base will be online. Have to love these old stations; all the same and got to love the lowest bidders."

"Good, Mr. Smith," Martinez answered and walked out to his left, followed by the bearded man, and the remaining group including one dark-haired woman in her thirties filed out to the right, all wearing black jumpsuits and black military boots, no insignias, and she was wearing miner's clothing, with a green nylon jacket. Mr. Smith remained behind collecting his equipment as the door closed.

The door to Command opened as Martinez approached and he stepped up to the center console, "When will the rest of your men be here, Mr. Jones?"

"Two days," Mr. Jones replied, scratching his beard, moving around to the forward console; the door opened again. Mr. Smith entered with his black-and-gray backpack. Martinez stood up and allowed him to sit.

"Get communications online, so I may contact our friends," Martinez ordered.

Mr. Smith took out his screen again, and laid it on the console, connecting two separate cables into the console, tapped a few times, the console lit up, and he laid the screen down.

"*Trinity* activated and awaiting orders," *Gamma* said.

"I told Nagoya that we should never use a female's voice on military bases or stations, or any space vessel for that matter, delete that damn thing," Martinez ordered.

Mr. Smith ran his fingers over the console, "Done, not hearing her again, now with *the Roosevelt* jamming this sector of space, we are all alone."

"Good, will *your* squad be ready by the time the second squad is here?" Martinez asked Mr. Jones.

"Yes," he replied standing from the chair, he was lounging in, and walking out.

Martinez looked out the window at the desolate moon, thinking. Then turned back, "How long till I can speak to our friends?"

Mr. Smith tapped his screen and pulled off the Velcro strap over his watch, "Twenty minutes."

"Good, contact *the Roosevelt* then and have them stop jamming," Martinez ordered as he left.

Mr. Smith leaned down and picked his pack up off the deck, placing it on the console, and pulled out a small radio with headphones. Putting the headphones on, pulled a soda bottle from his pack, leaned back, turned his radio on, and started listening to his tunes.

The young woman with her hair up in a ponytail now was lying down on her back, under a console in one of the cargo bays with two kits open and different tools and cables on either side of her. There were also cables hanging down from the console above her, which she was reaching up inside, searching for something. Two other men with very short military haircuts, one with red hair, the other with dark hair, both in their mid-thirties and moving equipment, large cylinder tubes, and crates into a large shuttle's rear cargo hold, with its door raised in line with the roof of the shuttle.

Mr. Jones entered from the far end, opposite the console, and looked over at the men, and grunted, "Hurry up," they stopped and looked back at him, then continued with their work. He stepped up to the console, "Ms. Green, are we on schedule?"

"I will need six hours to remove one of the power cores and move it to a shuttle before we head down, once I am done here," Ms. Green replied from under the console without looking up.

"What are you doing there?"

She shifted from under the console, leaning up on her elbows with disgust in her voice, because he had interrupted her again, as he does many times, and spoke very slowly for him, "I learned someone had placed a homing device in this console when the base was deactivated.

If I do not finish, whoever did put it in, will find us, and I don't think our employers would like that."

He shook his head, shrugged his shoulders, and wiped his hands, as if to wash his hands of her, "Just get it done," and stormed out.

She mouthed sarcastically, "Get it done," as a child would, then stuck her tongue out and returned up under the console to her work. The two men loading the shuttle stopped and laughed, "I hope you are having fun, gentlemen. I do not think our employers will be too happy with the payments they are providing you if they knew you were goofing off and not loading *their* shuttles," she yelled across the room without getting up, as if a Mother scolding her children.

Martinez was now in the medical bay and catching some shut eye as Mr. Jones entered, "Ms. Green found a homing beacon attached to a shuttle bay console and is now removing it."

Martinez sat up, "I thought I had removed all of them when I left, six years ago," as he jumped off the bed, "How long till the power core is on the shuttle?"

"Ms. Green needs six hours once she has removed the homing beacon."

"Damn. . . that could put us behind by three hours," his watch beeped; he undid the Velcro, "Let's go, time to inform our friends."

Mr. Smith still leaning back in the chair, one leg resting on the console, bobbing his head, and dancing to the music, with three empty soda bottles on the deck and a half-eaten tuna sandwich resting on wax paper on the console, with his eyes closed.

The door opened, and Martinez saw the mess this boy had made and was furious. Slapping the headphones off his head, "I have been gone only fifteen minutes, and you have trashed this place!"

Mr. Smith quickly sat up and scrambled, grabbing up the bottles, crammed them into his backpack, took another bite of the tuna sandwich and folded the paper up, shoved it into his backpack, and wiped the crumbs off the console.

Martinez walked around the console, looked down at Mr. Smith with disgust, and then back up at Mr. Jones with an expression of the merits of his crew.

"Best tech, I found for the price."

Martinez turned back to Mr. Smith and started tapping his finger on the top edge of the console, impatiently.

Mr. Smith quickly wiped the console again, taking his headphones and radio off, and putting them away. Running his fingers over the console quickly, and looked up past Martinez, as the window melted into a vid screen.

Two men and one woman sat at a table across the room on the vid screen; one of the men sitting in the center Martinez knew, Senator Cooper. The woman was sitting to his right he did not know. She is African, in her late thirties, wearing a gray business suit, with short black hair. The other man was tall, even for sitting, to Cooper's left, a white man in his fifties, completely bald, wearing a white dress shirt and red tie.

Martinez was not pleased with the others involved since he did not know them, "Orrin? Who are your friends?"

Cooper leaned forward and scanned the room, "I could ask you the same question, Miguel?" as he looked from Mr. Smith and then Mr. Jones, not remembering they were the two men who entered the room on *IO* with him.

Martinez looked at his men, then back at the screen, "Worth their pay."

Cooper gestured to the man on his left, "Mr. Rudolph, of Earth, an exceptionally good financer of our cause. and this is Ms. King, of Mars, another exceptionally good benefactor," as he introduced them.

Martinez just smiled, because all he heard was money, money, money, and the sound of coins rattling.

"We need to keep this short, any longer than two minutes and the *Gamma II* station will have an Uplink to Earth," Mr. Smith advised.

"Yes, the summit on Mars is set for oh-nine hundred hours, Mars Zulu, Founders Dome, fifteen days from now, I do hope you will be done by then and we will have no more problems with *Gamma II*," Cooper explained.

Martinez shot a look at Mr. Jones, each knowing they were a bit behind schedule, now that Ms. Green found a homing beacon and putting them behind schedule. He turned back toward the screen, "Should be. . ."

Cooper just looked at him across the vid screen, questioning.

"Times up," Mr. Smith said, and the screen went black.

"Good, I was getting tired of that asshole," Martinez said.

Over the COM, came Ms. Green, "Mr. Jones, you need to see something I found, I am on my way to Engineering to get the power core, meet me there." Martinez nodded, and he left.

"Can we make contact with my man on *Gamma II*, now?"

"Yes," Mr. Smith answered and pressed a single button on the console, opening a lower frequency channel outside the jammer's range, "Bravo six, Bravo twelve, come in, over. Bravo six, Bravo twelve come in, over," Mr. Smith repeated.

A long pause, "Bravo twelve, Bravo six, over," Adams replied.

Smith pointed with his hand toward Martinez and then down at the console.

"Alpha one here, report, over."

"A friendly here willing to help, target is still looking into the code, but no luck yet, over."

Martinez knew the friendly was Hitchcock because they both had history and Martinez was the one who stationed him on *Gamma II* as the second in Command after Macpherson was assigned, against all his protests and outranked by Vice Admiral Wainwright, "We should be planet side in seven hours, over."

"Understood, over."

"I now, wish to talk with our target alone, once there, over," Martinez ordered.

"Yes, over. . .Got to go, over," then just static. Mr. Smith closed the channel.

Entering Engineering, Mr. Jones saw Ms. Green waiting, she turned toward him and handed him a small flat card. He just looked at it, shrugging his shoulders. Confirming what she had always thought of him, he was just muscle, no brains. *Another asshole*, she thought. She took it back and slid it into a slot on the console's top, "Data files."

The small monitor screen activated in the center of the upper section of the console and began to spit out data, and she told him to read it, knowing he probably could not.

Data begins scrolling up the screen, "Something about *the Andromeda System*, a mission, and a new device. . ." he stopped her in midsentence, as he yanked the disk from the slot, and ran out.

Mr. Jones rushed into Command, trying to catch his breath, and waving the disk, "You. . . have to see. . . this," and slid it into the slot on the console that Mr. Smith was still at, and the window melted into a computer screen. The same data in Engineering scrolled up.

In a flash, Martinez turned to the two men and snapped his fingers, pointing at the door. "Out! Get out!"

CHAPTER FIVE

CONSPIRACY

VICE ADMIRAL ANDREW JACKSON WAINWRIGHT sat behind a large metallic rectangular desk, which looked more like an old-fashioned oak desk of the twentieth century. His office resided at the interstellar scientific research station on the *Tharsis plateau*, Mars, part of the Earth Alliance Admiralty. He was in his sixties, with salt-and-pepper hair and wearing a pair of brown-and-gold-framed reading glasses that rested barely on his nose. He was wearing his white dress uniform, slack with a long-sleeved white shirt, three gold stars were on his epaulets, and he was a veteran of Mars Military Command and was going over the daily reports for the two weeks, after returning from a vacation on his island home on Earth. His aide, a young Lieutenant, runs in, dark-haired in his late twenties, wearing a blue jumpsuit, and "Davidson" stitched across his left chest pocket, he handed the Admiral a black folder, "Sir, you need to look at this."

Admiral Wainwright looked up over his glasses, "What is it, Lieutenant?"

"We just learned *Gamma II* has gone dark, no contact for the last two months, and they have missed their last three check-ins."

Taking the folder, the Admiral glanced through it, "Any atmospheric or background radiation in the area that could cause this disruption?" he asked without looking up.

"No, Sir."

He waved him out, holding the folder in his left hand, and taking his glasses off, placing the left earpiece in his mouth, and pondered it all.

Walked over to the large nearly panoramic window, left of his desk, tapped on the ledge below the window, and the vid screen activated. A mature, thick dark-haired man with some gray and wearing eagles on his epaulets of his blue short-sleeved shirt, and his nameplate read "Walker,"

Yes, Sir."

"Captain, what is this I just heard, there has been no communication with the *Gamma II* station?"

The Captain paused and shifted in his chair then picked up a black folder.

"Yes, Sir. They have missed their last three Uplinks."

The Admiral raised his right hand, still holding the black folder he had received for Davidson. He had never trusted this man and had known for a time; that he was in cahoots with Martinez.

"Captain, and I use that title for the moment, I have that report . . . what else can you tell me? You are in communications, correct?" Admiral Wainwright knew whatever he told him was a lie.

Walker was taken back a bit, "I am sorry, Sir. That is all we have at present."

The Admiral slammed his hand down on the console, and the screen went black, "Davidson!"

The Lieutenant returned and the Admiral started pacing the small area of his beige rug, "Find me the most recent reports on *Gamma II*, within the last six months for Mars, Earth, and *IO*." The Lieutenant snapped to attention and headed out.

The Admiral turned back to the console, and typed, this time a Commodore, a single-star gentleman in his sixties, bald, and sitting at his desk.

"Jack, how the hell have you been?"

"Hal, I have a major issue here, we have not heard from *Gamma II* for two weeks, which you know is like two months by the time the communication gets here, have you heard anything?"

"No, but my efforts have been on the new mining drill for the deep ocean core. Sorry, Jack, I have been overseeing inner space for the last two years here on Earth, at the Inner Space Research Center, at Diamond Head, Hawaii."

"Thanks, I forgot your transfer," he replied as he closed the channel, walked back to his desk, and picked up a small screen that was lying there, and tapped it a couple of times.

GAMMA II—ENVIRONMENTAL AND
CLIMATIALOGIC RESEARCH STATION

ESTABLISHED SEPTEMBER 15, 2273,
CAPTAIN REBECCA MACPHERSON—
GEOPHYSICAL SCIENTIST, AND
OPERATIONAL COMMANDER EARTH
ALLIANCE

STATATION 132—CREW COMPLIMENT 8

"I already know this, I assigned her there," he typed more.
The Screen displays.

GAMMA II QUARANTINED
Admiral F. M. Martinez, 2263

"I lifted that quarantine, a year ago. Why can't I find anything before I assigned Macpherson, or now!"

He typed: REAR ADMIRAL F. M. MARTINEZ----the screen flashed red:

CLASSIFIED

He looked down at the screen with shock, "I am a three-star Vice Admiral, and this is classified to me. Classified!" Tossed the screen on his desk, walked back to the vid screen, and tapped again.

Senator Orrin Cooper appeared, behind his desk, on Capitol Hill, looking puzzled that Admiral Wainwright was calling him, "Jack? What can I do for you?"

"Orrin, why is all data on Admiral Martinez and *Gamma II* classified?"

Cooper overtly bit his bottom lip, "Got me, Jack, I have no idea, have not talked to Miguel for weeks. Last I heard, he was on vacation back home in Veracruz, since he retired, does not wish to be contacted, and I heard he went native."

Admiral Wainwright knew this was a line of bull. Anyone in the inner circle of the military knew they were in bed together, "If you do hear anything, or from him, you will let me know?"

Cooper shrugged his shoulders and smiled. "Sure, Jack, you'll be the first," Cooper tapped a button on his desk just a bit off-screen and closed the vid screen.

The vid screen changed again to an image of Admiral Nagoya, she was now retired and in civilian clothing, with an apron, working in her small kitchen, somewhere in Japan, "Jack, good morning, long time."

"I am truly sorry to bother you, Tatsumi, but I seem to have a mystery here, and hoping you could assist?"

She looked back with puzzlement, "If I can,"

"Before you retired, do you remember anything new with Martinez and *Gamma II?*"

She thought for a moment, "He was not happy with how that ended, and the loss of Bowers and it pissed him off. Recently, he had been on very private, long trips to Mars and *IO*, and never documented a thing. Once, he even went to Russia and told everyone it was a vacation, but I learned later he was meeting with Professor Ranko," she paused, "Then three months ago, six months after he retired, he just disappeared."

"Off the record, would you know of any reason why *I* would be locked out of any files regarding him or *Gamma II?*"

She stood there for a moment, then looked around, and then moved a bit closer to the vid screen, "Jack, I was also cut out of everything after that meeting with Bowers about *Gamma II*, thirteen years ago." She looked around again, "And I tell you, he is up to something, and that bastard, Orrin is in on it too, and that is off the record." They looked at each other for a moment. "Watch your back, Jack," she said in a whisper and touched a button closing the vid.

Davidson returned holding a screen with puzzlement on his face, "Sir? All the files you have requested are flagged classified and need a level-one Omega clearance."

Admiral Wainwright grabbed the screen from the Lieutenant, with disgust, "Why a war command for this!" He tapped out his code, the Omega clearance, and the screen flashed red, and CLASSIFIED. The Lieutenant could tell the Admiral was now pissed. The Admiral waved him off again, and he left.

He tossed the screen down, hard, "Shit!" He knew now Martinez was up to something, but what? Every door he tried was slammed shut, hard in his face, not normal for the Vice Admiral of Mars Military Affairs and Planetary Scientific Research.

If he could not go through normal channels, there was always a back door, "I have a few markers out there, and it's time to collect." He gathered up a few other folders and put the black folder into an old-style brown leather case, which was sitting on the top left corner of his desk, clasped the flap on the front, and left himself.

Senator Maxwell Macomb's early-nineteenth-century Victorian four-story home sat atop a hill in the Macomb district of Mars. Macomb was one of only a few Senators on the apparitions committee for the Mars Assembly and worked closely with the Admiralty.

The estate was brought to Mars, brick by brick, window by window, keeping it complete in the style of one of his ancestors on Earth, in Southern Georgia on the North American continent. Macomb could trace his family back to before the American Civil War; one of the first Commanders of the exploration ships to Mars back in the early twenty-first century was a Macomb.

Admiral Wainwright thought it was too elaborate for this backwater community of *Mars* as he stood waiting on the oversized porch, as the Sun slowly set behind the house. A tall well-dressed African American man in his sixties, in a tuxedo, answered the door, "Yes?"

"Vice Admiral Andrew Jackson Wainwright, to see Senator Macomb?"

He nodded, stepped back, and allowed the Admiral to enter, closing the door, then motions to take the Admiral's case, but the Admiral declined, "Please, follow me, Sir?"

They walked across the grand and elegant foyer, two long spiral staircases leading upstairs, on each side, and a simple round table with a fern plant resting atop and with a white sheet hanging down off the table. They step up to a set of rolling double doors. The Butler slid them open, a large late-nineteenth-century library.

Admiral Wainwright had been here before, and still found this room pathetic; shelves of books running nearly two stories high, *people use computer screens nowadays for a good book*, he thought, with a small terrace along the second floor, with a metal rolling ladder along the back wall. A small circular staircase in the far-right corner and a large white marble fireplace sat inside the room across from the sliding doors.

Two large high-back chairs, one white, one brown, sat in the middle, each with ottomans, a table and a glass vase, a light brown liquid inside, and a few glasses on a silver and glass tray. Off to the far right, an oversized Louis the XIV desk with elegant designs and carvings, "You may wait here, Sir," the Butler said, backing out of the room slowly, and sliding the doors closed.

Macomb was always a pompous ass, he thought as he looks over the room, walked up to the table, dropped his case into the brown chair to his left, and tipped the vase back, for a better look. "Still a bourbon man, I see," then stepped to the oversized white marble fireplace, with a roaring fire, warming the room, and ran his right index finger along the top, and found no dust.

A first-edition hardback bound Huckleberry Finn rested on the mantle as the doors rolled open breaking his concentration.

Senator Maxwell Macomb, tall, with red hair, a bit over six foot, and with a beard, he brown-tweeted gentleman's suit of the late nineteenth century. He was leaning in holding both doors, "Jack, Jack, Jack, how long has it been?" with a slight New Orleans Creole accent, as the Butler closed the doors behind him. Admiral Wainwright turned toward him. They shook hands and Macomb moved to the table, opened the vase, "Care for some, Jack?" and started to pour drinks.

"This is not a social call, Max!"

Macomb turned back with puzzlement, put the vase down, and sat down across from him, "Then?"

Admiral Wainwright moved behind the other large chair, "It's time to pay the piper, Max," Macomb leaned forward still with confusion.

Admiral Wainwright knew Macomb knew why he was here as he started to open his case, "I need to know what all you know about Admiral Martinez's recent ongoings and *Gamma II's* happenings in the last six months. I think, he is up to his old tricks again," he explained, and sat down.

Macomb fell back into the chair, intertwined his fingers over his chest, looked down at the floor, and let out a heavy sigh, and knowing that Admiral Wainwright would not ask this unless he had a good reason. He stood up quickly, poured himself a double, and drank it down, fast, "Officially or Unofficially?"

Admiral Wainwright slumped back into the large high back chair, knowing from his reaction, that this was not going to be good, "Unofficially?" knowing it would be the truth.

Macomb's face turned white, and he leaned over the other high back chair that he was just sitting in, "Bowers is alive and on *Gamma II!*"

The bright rays of the Sun shined into Admiral Wainwright's office; he tossed his case on a chair behind his desk. Davidson followed him in, "Take the rest of the day off, Son."

Davidson looked at him with puzzlement. Admiral Wainwright looked up at him with a strong glare, "You deef, Mister?"

Davidson snapped to attention and rushed out. Admiral Wainwright tapped on one of the two screens still on his desk and then stepped over to the window, tapping the ledge. Captain Walker reappeared, "Yes, Admiral?"

"Any *new* reports on *Gamma II?*" already knowing the answer.

Walker sat there, not too sure what to do, and turned away briefly, then back, shuffled a few files, and opened the same black folder from yesterday, "No, Sir."

Admiral Wainwright rolled his eyes, and let out a heavy sigh, shook his head, looked down at the floor, and pinched the bridge of his nose. He had been in this man's military all his adult life, had raised three kids, and knew when someone was lying right to his face, and he knew right then that Walker was covering for Martinez. He stepped forward, slammed the ledge, and closed the channel.

Martinez was holding all the cards, and he needed someone he could trust. He took a deep breath, regained his composure, and tapped a few more times. A young African American woman, in her early forties, with silver oak leaves on her epaulets, "Admiral, how may I assist you?"

"Commander, can you tell me what ships are in the area near the *Triton System?*"

She leaned forward, typing, "Yes, Sir, here we go. *The Theodore Roosevelt* is closest but is on a classified mission and running silent. *The Churchill, the Roanoke,* and *the Crazy Horse* are two systems away, near *Orion Six.*"

He felt better, the Commander was able to give him answers, unlike the Captain, "Thank you, Commander, you have been a big help."

"Glad to be of service, Admiral. Is there anything thing else, Sir?"

"No." The screen went black and slowly melted back into the plateau with the morning Sun rays shining in. He swiped his hand across the window, and a set of blinds lowered He knew now Martinez was there. *The Roosevelt* was his flagship, and if he contacted them, that would be a dead end. The crew would follow Martinez into hell and back without question. The Admiral finally had a trump card of his own. He knew the Captain of *the Roanoke* personally, and he could trust her. The Captain of *the Roanoke* was his own daughter, Jessica Wainwright.

* * *

The Roanoke, was a larger-size science research vessel, twice the size of *the Gore,* and hovering in orbit above the desert planet of a colony world outside *the Sol System.* One of the first colonies, in the late 2260s, in a small system on a second arm of the *Milky Way Galaxy,* six planets, three terrestrial and three gas giants, but only one habitable. *Orion Six* is a desert world with little water and one northern pole. The atmosphere was brown and orange in color. with her two other smaller science vessels, *the Churchill,* and *the Crazy Horse* resting alongside in a high orbit.

Captain Jessica Wainwright sat in her quarters, in a blue jumpsuit, behind an elongated oblong glass tabletop, with a small celestial globe in the upper right-hand corner. Four hard-cover back bound books stand on the left corner in between two white marble bookends shaped like horses, various knickknacks, and books in a four-shelf unit behind her, set into the wall. Sitting on the second shelf, right off center are two pictures, facing one another, one of her Father, and the other, of her and Bowers. They were standing together on a beach, in a loving embrace. He was wearing a pair of long black swim trunks and green aviator glasses. She was dressed in a blue bikini with a blue wrap around her thighs and had dark sunglasses on. Her blonde hair was lying down just past her shoulders, each in their mid-twenties and looking very loving and happy, a special time for them both.

Two small screens on her desk, one right in front of her and the other off to her left near the opposite end. She was holding a third, looking over reports, and then walked over to the small coffee table, glass, and brass frame, two more leather-bound books resting on the table, with a silver pitcher of coffee, three silver mugs rested on a silver, brass, and glass tray, with black handles on either end. She poured some coffee from the pitcher into the cup she was carrying. An adjacent room, off to the left of her desk, an archway separating the rooms, and two large windows behind the coffee table, above a long white couch against the wall.

"Captain, Admiral Wainwright is on subspace," *Gamma* reported.

Jessica Wainwright smiled, "I'll take it here," as she crossed the room, back to her desk, to a panel on the wall behind it, next to her shelf unit, a few buttons, and a good-size vid screen, she pressed one, and Admiral Wainwright appeared, "Daddy — Sir."

He smiled back, "I need your help, Princess." *He never called, to just talk anymore,* she thought. But when he needed something, he called her Princess, "Are you done with your mission at *Orion Six?*"

"Just finished, helping the colonist repair their global satellites, an aqueduct, and then onto *Andromeda.*"

"Good, I need to augment your mission orders, I am reassigning you, *the Crazy Horse* and *the Churchill* will complete your current assignment in the *Andromeda Galaxy.*"

"Yes, and *the Roanoke?*"

"We have lost all contact with *Gamma II* in the *Triton System;* they have not checked in for a couple of months. Macpherson is normally prompt, and with them less than twenty days before their atmosphere changes, to dangerous levels of carbon dioxide. I need you to find out what happened; I hope it is just a communications glitch, and FYI, Princess. Admiral Martinez has disappeared, but *the Roosevelt* is in the area, he has in the past pushed for some reason to not allow others on the planets, so be careful. Do not contact the *Roosevelt* when in range, I know he is there, somewhere, and I know you remember his backroom dealings, he used to play," She nodded, recalling all the problems Bowers had with him.

"Yes," The vid screen went black. She looked at his picture, "And tell Mom I miss her too," then toward the other one, picked it up, and looked tenderly at the two of them on the beach. She missed him and still loved him, dearly, and she was wearing the ring he had on *the Clinton.*

Gamma II was where he disappeared. She wished there had been more time, and she knew he was going to ask her to marry her again, and she would have said yes this time. She wiped the tears from her eyes, placed the picture back on the shelf, and straightened her jumpsuit.

"Computer, alert the senior staff to report to the conference room, immediately."

"Yes, Ma'am," *Gamma* replied, as she turned and exited her quarters.

Lieutenant Commander Donavan and Lieutenant Galloway enter the conference room, where Jessica Wainwright is waiting, a long conference table, black with six high-back chairs on each side, and one at each end. Donavan, a tall young blonde man in his mid-thirties, wearing a green jumpsuit, and the ship's Doctor, sits on the far side of the table, on Jessica Wainwright's right.

Lieutenant Galloway, a young twenty-something woman, with dark hair, and wearing a yellow jumpsuit, the ship's Communications officer, joined the Doctor. Donavan leaned over the table, picked up a glass, and poured some water from the pitcher that was resting in the center of the table.

All looked up as Commander Watson entered, in his late forties, with black hair, and a scar down his right cheek from a confrontation with Admiral Martinez years earlier and wearing a blue jumpsuit. Chief Engineer Commander Hoffman followed Watson in, an African American man in his fifties, in a yellow jumpsuit, sat down next to Watson.

Jessica Wainwright leaned forward a bit in her chair, "I have just received new orders from the Admiralty, we are to report to *Gamma II* and find out why they have gone dark and have not reported in for a couple of months."

"Our mission to *Andromeda* canceled?" Watson asked.

"No, just delayed. The *Crazy Horse* and *the Churchill* will continue with the present assignment. Hoffman and Galloway, please put together teams to assist *Gamma II's* personnel, with Communications and any Engineering, and Environmental needs." Hoffman and Galloway nodded and quickly stepped out.

Jessica Wainwright walked around the table nearest the Doctor, "Computer, secure room and pause all recordings."

"Room secured, Ma'am, and all recording devices off," *Gamma* replied.

"I know Commander Watson will agree with me that Admiral Martinez cannot be trusted." Jessica Wainwright said, Watson had a stern look on his face.

"Jessica?" Donavon asked.

"I said the Admiralty to the others, but really it was my Father who contacted me, and informed me of *Gamma II* and that Martinez was in the area, and that something was up."

Watson shifted in his chair, uncomfortably, "You think we may have trouble with him?" Watson asked.

"I don't really know, but *the Roosevelt* has been reported in the area." She answered him, the Doctor let out a heavy sigh. "To let you both know, ten years ago, Martinez quarantined *Gamma II* and later we heard he wanted it for his own purposes," Jessica Wainwright said.

"He's a walking nightmare if you ask me Ma'am, and if he is here, there is a conspiracy afoot." Watson added, "The ship will be ready for anything, Captain."

"Captain, my sensors are detecting a small shuttlecraft on a direct course toward us, at a high speed," *Gamma* reported.

"Thank you," she looked at Watson, who nodded and exited.

"He called you Princess. right?" Donovan asked. She nodded and sat down. Jessica Wainwright and Donavan have both known Bowers for many years. They were in the academy together, in Command College, and both men knew her family very well, "Then we are in for one hell of a mess," he said with his strong Texas accent, "Anything else?"

"No."

"The small shuttle is sending a class one, Omega priority to dock, Ma'am," *Gamma* advised.

"War," Donovan said.

"Notify shuttle bay two and acknowledge the signal, Computer." Jessica Wainwright ordered.

Jessica Wainwright, Watson, and four others in yellow jumpsuits holding small vacuum pistols, palm size, waited as the tractor beam slowly glided the shuttle into the bay, and rested it gently on the cargo bay deck; a force field was holding back the vacuum of space. Watson was also holding a vacuum pistol, two security members behind him, and the two others behind Jessica Wainwright, also waiting for whatever or whoever was inside.

The shuttle's small hatch slowly rose as Watson and the two men behind him took up positions on either side of the hatch.

Professor Dmitri Ranko exited, wearing the same old brown suit from thirteen years ago, with almost no hair on his head, and a black toupee, which also looked like he had slept in it, he was also holding a black case. Seeing the two guards, he waited and looked around.

Jessica Wainwright recognized him and called out, "Dmitri," The men backed off, "Dmitri," she called out again and hugged him. Ranko slowly stepped forward and returned the hug.

"From your Father, Miss," as he opened his case and handed her a black folder. She skimmed it, quickly turned, and headed out.

"Conference room, now!" she ordered.

All funnel into the conference room. Ranko sat immediately across the room from the door, with two of the four guards behind him while the remaining two stopped just inside. Watson sat across from Ranko.

Jessica Wainwright waved at the four guards, "Outside! Computer, secure room and pause all recordings."

"Captain, I take it you can vouch for this man, I presume?" Watson asked.

She nodded, handing the black folder to Watson, "As does my Father, the Admiral. Professor Ranko is here to inform us of new information, and what is going on with Martinez, the Admiral has learned more, and hopefully, we will not go into this blindly. Professor, if you, please?" Jessica Wainwright said as she sat.

"I have known Admiral Martinez for many years and thirteen years ago, he and I, along with Senator Cooper and Admiral Nagoya, informed Commander Bowers of *the Triton System* and *Gamma II*. Bowers was to travel to *Gamma II* and investigate more about why it was a desert world, no longer fertile as it was just twenty years prior, and why the atmosphere turns to carbon dioxide, like Venus. For two hundred and fifty days as it is closest to the Sun, and only takes forty-eight hours to complete the process from oxygen atmosphere to the carbon dioxide, and if it was a good site for colonization," Ranko explained, "Once Bowers arrived, word came down that he was dead. Martinez quarantined the planet and classified all knowledge of it."

"So why is he here now?" Watson asked.

Ranko took a deep breath, a long pause, and let it out slowly and then looked at Jessica Wainwright, "Your Father has learned Martinez has put together a team of mercenaries, staging first on *the Trinity* moon and then going to a second station on *Gamma II*, which only a few and Martinez know of."

"But why is he here, now!" Watson asked again, raising his voice.

Ranko looked down at the table, tapped his fingers nervously around his case, and then slowly looked up toward Jessica Wainwright, "Bowers is alive and on *Gamma II*."

CHAPTER SIX

AWAKENED

ALARMS RANG OUT, RED LIGHTS FLASHED. "Captain Macpherson to Command," *Gamma* called out. Running down the corridor toward Command, Macpherson nearly ran into Bowers at a junction. "What now!"

"Hell, if I know, I am just visiting," Bower said.

The door to Command opened, "Kill the alarms, *Gamma*!" Macpherson ordered.

Mitchell was working at the center console, "I am trying, most of her functions are offline," he yelled.

"Captain Macpherson to Command," *Gamma* called out again.

"What's happening?" Macpherson yelled as the alarms cut off.

"Some of *Gamma's* daily routine functions are still corrupted," Mitchell answered, "When they ran, the station reported an oxygen leak in the central hub, and notified you as policy deems," Mitchell answered.

"I thought Walker-Swanson had a handle on this?" Macpherson asked, as Mitchell and Bowers just looked at each other and then back at her, "All right, all right, I'll find Walker-Swanson myself," as she left Bowers and Mitchell in Command.

Walker-Swanson ran up the corridor and nearly slammed into Macpherson, as she was finishing dressing, "What happened, Ma'am?"

The Captain braced herself as Walker-Swanson slammed into her, landing both on the deck, and she helped the Captain up, "It seems not all the files needed, the daily functions, were fixed." Macpherson advised.

What?"

"Some files are still corrupted, *Gamma* was running her daily routine functions, and the system reported an oxygen leak in the central hub and called me to Command. Mitchell was able to finally kill the alarms and find the issue."

"I am sorry, Ma'am, I thought I had fixed the data, especially life support, but with all that is going on, and *him* being here, I —"

Cutting her off, with a raised hand, "Commander Bowers is here, and shit is happening, deal with it! We need to fix *Gamma* and find out why we cannot contact Earth. Can you do that, Lieutenant?"

Shaking her head, "Yes, Ma'am."

Macpherson continued into the medical bay, leaving Walker-Swanson standing there, "Remy, I got a headache this big," with her hands apart a few centimeters.

Doctor Mabuto laughed and put his hands on her shoulders, "It will be okay, Bekka."

She laid her head on his chest, "I just want to crawl up in a corner somewhere and hide."

Calvin shifted on the bed, "Where am I?"

"It's okay, Son, how are you feeling?" Mabuto asked as they joined him.

"Better, what happened?"

"You gave us a scare, John," Macpherson said, "Thought we lost you."

"Yeah, so I died?"

"Sorry to say it, Son, but yes," Mabuto answered.

Calvin tried to sit up but could not, and he looked over at the Doctor curiously, "Why the restraints, Doc?"

"I have had too many leaving my medical bay recently, and not being able to do a complete workup, not going to have that happen again. A complete scan of Mr. Calvin, please, *Gamma?*"

Calvin looked at Macpherson and mouthed, "Who?"

"Just follow the Doctor's orders, Calvin, I will explain later."

Alarms rang out. Red lights flashed, Walker-Swanson and Mitchell were in Engineering working at the center console, and Adams was standing at the back near the far wall, and finally able to turn the alarms off, "Everything looks normal," Mitchell commented.

Adams pushed his way through, shoving Mitchell to the floor, "Out of my way, kid!"

Walker-Swanson stooped down near Mitchell, "Hey!"

"You too, Bitch! Both of you get the Hell out of my Engineering!"

Helping Mitchell to his feet, as Bowers stepped up to Engineering, they exited and met just outside, as the door closed behind them, "What happened?" Bowers asked.

"That Bastard just kicked us out of Engineering," Walker-Swanson said, irritated.

"I mean what's with the alarms?"

"Hell, if I know, the three of us were trying to find out why the alarms were sounding off again, and he kicked us out," Walker-Swanson answered.

Before Bowers could answer, Hitchcock came from behind him, "I will find out," and brushed him aside, and out of the way, and continued into Engineering.

"Command now, both of you, maybe you can learn something there," Bowers ordered. Walker-Swanson hesitated and then followed Mitchell. Bowers started toward Engineering but saw a black-cloaked figure out of the corner of his eye running down the hallway, past him. He turned fast and started after it, down one corridor, turned right, stopped abruptly at a dead end, and watched as the black-cloaked figure ran out across the desert.

Macpherson tapped his shoulder, "What you are looking at?"

He jumped, "Don't do that... You wouldn't believe me if I told you."

She crossed in front of him, still looking out the window, "The desert?"

"A black-cloaked figure over three meters tall passed through this wall, and ran out there," as he pointed at the window.

"Has Doc been giving you one of his blue pills?"

He looked at her, "I know what I saw!"

"With all that is going on, I wouldn't doubt it."

"Blue pills you say?" Bowers questioned.

Swanson entered the medical bay, and continued up to Calvin and the Doctor, as Calvin finished dressing, "How's he doing?"

"Better, I have put him on light duty for now."

"There is nothing light about what's been going on lately," Swanson said as Calvin just looked up at them with confusion, "Doc, where did you put the black cloak, the Captain found in the shuttle?"

The Doctor walked over to one of the drawers on the far wall, opened it, looked down, and backed up into the mirror with confusion, "Now, I know I put it right there."

Swanson stepped up behind him and looked down, seeing the empty draw, and then at him through the mirror, "I'd better inform the Captain."

"Yes, definitely, you should," Mabuto said as she left quickly.

Calvin stepped down near the Doctor, and looked over his shoulder, the Doctor returned to his console, pondering if he was losing his mind.

Alarms rang out. Red lights flashed. Macpherson slammed her fist down on the conference table, "What the fuck, now?"

Bowers entered, "You gotta see this."

All containers crates, and anything that was not nailed down was suspended in mid-air, as they entered the cargo bay, including the shuttle, then it all came crashing down, and the alarm cut off, "This never happened when I was stationed on *Mars*, during and after the riots," Macpherson commented.

Swanson and Calvin ran in, yelling at the same time, "Captain, you got to see this."

Macpherson looked at Bowers, "This place was quiet as a church, till *you* showed up!"

He shrugged his shoulders, and they ran after them.

All four ran into the pumping station, the pool was boiling over, and steam rising, from the hot water flowing across the floor, Mitchell was up on the catwalk above the pool, trying hard to turn a wrench, trying to close the valve for the pool, but unsuccessful.

Macpherson shook her head again, "What the fuck is going on here?"

A loud howling shriek as if a wounded animal cried out, and in a flash, the water on the floor was gone, the black-cloaked figure darted from their far right, into their line of sight, and toward the back wall, behind the pool. Bowers and Macpherson took off in a flash and nearly slammed into the back wall, and she turned toward Bowers, "I am getting tired of this. . ."

"I think you're right; I did wake something up."

All but Hitchcock and Chief Adams were sitting in the conference room, "Did we see what we just saw?" Swanson asked.

"I am starting to believe with the technology of the force field around the Pyramid, and the age of it, Ancient. I might have awoken something up ten years ago, but what I woke up, I don't know," Bowers explained, they all looked at him as if he had lost his mind, "With all that is going on, and other than the EM pulse affecting *Gamma*, your guess is as good as mine?"

"For now, let's put that on the back burner," Macpherson stated.

"We have rechecked the files and command systems, and repaired another small percentage of the corrupted files, which is now down to ten, the system is now working. *Gamma* should not have any more errors like the oxygen leak again unless there is one," Walker-Swanson advised.

"Can we fix the rest?" Macpherson asked.

"Not without an Uplink, I have found the system is working, but no connection with Earth or *Mars*," Mitchell added, "from what I can tell, it is not a system error, we are being jammed. Until Hitchcock and

Adams finish what they are doing in Engineering, I cannot look into it further."

Macpherson tapped the table, "Engineering, report? Mr. Hitchcock, Mr. Adams report?"

"Neither Chief Adams nor Command Hitchcock are present on the Station, Ma'am," Gamma answered.

Macpherson pointed at the door, "Mitchell, Engineering, fix that Uplink. Walker-Swanson, go with him."

"Now we have two missing crewmembers, it's getting better by the minute," Bowers commented.

Macpherson did not appreciate his comment, "So, where is the cloak, I ask for Ensign?"

"Doctor Mabuto showed me the drawer that he put it in, but it was no longer there."

"Remy?" Macpherson asked turning toward him.

"I am sorry, Bekka."

"The cloaked figure I saw passing through the window and then vanishing in the pumping station, is wearing it," Bowers said somewhat jokingly.

Macpherson looked down at the table and then back up at him, she was still not sure what she had seen or what was going on, but his jokes were not helping.

Mitchell was now kneeling near the keypad at Engineering with a screen and two cables, connected up inside the panel. He tapped the screen a few times, Walker-Swanson behind him, as Macpherson and Bowers joined them, "Report?" Macpherson ordered.

"Ma'am, the door is magnetically locked from the inside and Mitchell is trying to release it," Walker-Swanson said.

"Doors can only be magnetically sealed with the senior command codes," Bowers reminded her.

"Hitchcock and you, Ma'am, are the only ones that have those codes," Walker-Swanson added.

"*Gamma*, did Hitchcock give the order?" Macpherson asked.

"No, Ma'am, you did," *Gamma* answered. Macpherson looked from Walker-Swanson to Bowers.

"Got it," Mitchell said as he let the screen drop, dangling by the cables, the door snapped open, "Sir?" Bowers stepped up and they shoved the door the rest of the way opening it.

The lights were off except for a few that were still flickering, and smoke was heavy in the air, with sparks flying everywhere, Walker-Swanson jumped as the panel next to her sparked. Mitchell grabbed the flashlight off his tool belt and scanned the room, which was a mess.

"Lights," Macpherson called out, but nothing. Mitchell and Walker-Swanson hurried up the ramp to the main level, and Mitchell moved into a room behind the back wall. Macpherson flipped a couple of switches near the door and a few more lights came on. The room looked as if a bomb had gone off, the consoles and most panels on the walls were ripped out, cables everywhere and, still more smoke and sparks.

Mitchell returned from the back room, "We have another problem, Ma'am," he was holding an electronics board, "the Uplink circuit is dead."

"How long do you need for repairs?"

"This was the last board we had in storage, might be able to rig one from one of the shuttles," Mitchell answered.

"What the Hell did they do in here?" Walker-Swanson asked.

"*Gamma* any security logs after Hitchcock entered the room?" Macpherson asked.

"The monitor's stopped abruptly after Commander Hitchcock entered, Ma'am, " *Gamma* answered.

"I want to see those tapes in Command," then looked up at Walker-Swanson and Mitchell, "Do what you can." She turned, "With me, Mister."

On the vid screen in Command, Bowers, and Macpherson watched as Hitchcock entered, paused briefly, and looked up, his eyes glowing red, static appeared and cut to black, "Is that it, *Gamma?*" Macpherson asked.

"Yes, Ma'am."

"*Gamma* play it back again and hold when the Commander looks up," Bowers asked moving closer.

"You see something?"

"I think so," Bowers said as the vid screen started again and stopped as Hitchcock looked up with his eyes red, "Hold!"

Macpherson leaned forward, squinting for a better view, stepped around the console, and moved closer to the vid screen, "His eyes are red?"

"The same red eyes, I saw on Calvin before I was tossed across the room like a rag doll two days ago."

She turns back, "So we're not alone."

"Captain, you are needed in Environmental Control," Gamma reported.

Macpherson and Swanson entered Environmental Control, and the lights were off, each with a flashlight, and looking over the room, "Lights. . . Gamma, lights," But no reply.

Macpherson turned to her left, and touched a section of the wall, "Gamma, lights!"

The door closed fast behind them, and a loud howling shriek as if a wounded animal cried out. The room dropped down a long dark shaft, both screaming and for a moment both were floating in mid-air and then crashed hard onto the ground. A loud howling shriek as if a wounded animal cried out.

Bowers entered the medical bay, "Doc?" But no one was there. He started to leave, seeing the tall, black-cloaked figure blocking his way, with only his red eyes glowing from under the cowl, over three meters tall. Bowers could tell from the body frame under the cloak that it was humanoid as the figure raised his hands slowly. Red bolts of lightning erupted, as a windstorm began, in this controlled environment, and Bowers was tossed across the room and over one of the beds, slamming into the far back wall.

One of the overhead light units exploded, sparks flew everywhere, and then the console exploded with cables and debris flying everywhere, "I told you to get off my planet!" a low deep gravelly voice yelled through the windstorm, then as quickly as it started, it was over. Sparks fly from the console and light fixture; smoke rose as the cloak around the figure dropped.

Swanson ran in with Calvin, who was carrying a fire extinguisher. She tripped over the black cloak as Calvin used the extinguisher to put the fire out in the console. He dropped the extinguisher and helped Swanson up, they heard Bowers moving behind the bed, and both hurry, helping him up, "You all right, Sir?" Calvin asked.

"Yes," propping himself up on the bed.

Doctor Mabuto came in fast, "That thing nearly killed you!"

Calvin returned to the console, moved the extinguisher out of the way, pulled the chair back, which was across the room, and sat looking over the damage. Bowers stood, motioned to Swanson, that he was good, and walked over to the Doctor, who was now picking up the cloak, which Bowers took from him, "Bekka was right, I did wake something up."

CHAPTER SEVEN

THE LIE

MARTINEZ LEANED BACK IN THE CHAIR, as he looked over the vid screen, and pondered the data scrolling up. Someone had documented his mission plans for the *Andromeda Galaxy* and the experimental weapons, the three livable planets, the advanced technology, and the toys he brought back from his first mission.

"Mr. Jones reports the remaining squad will be here in less than two hours," Ms. Green advised.

He did not answer her at first, just slammed his fist on the console, and then turned around to see her.

"Mr. Jones reports the remaining squad will be here in less than two hours."

"Good, but we are three hours behind schedule unless you have found a way to speed up the process of getting me, *my* power core?"

"I only told Mr. Jones that to keep him away from me, he is an idiot, and keeps trying to hit on me. I am tired of his remarks," she explained.

Martinez giggled, walked over to her, took her by the hands, and looked at her deeply, "Pilar, my sweet Daughter. I knew I could always rely on you," in a Fatherly way, and then kissed her on the cheek.

The door slid open, and she moved back, and away trying to cover up the intimacy between her and her Father. Martinez looked sharply at Mr. Smith, who just stood there, looking as if he thought he had seen something, he should not have.

"What?" Martinez asked.

"Sir, it's time to make your last contact from here."

"Yes," Martinez pointed at the console.

Ms. Green left quickly, and Mr. Smith tapped a few times, the data from the disk disappeared and changed to a vid screen.

The President of Earth sat behind his desk in the Oval Office, with Rear Admiral Fitzsimmons. Mr. Smith's jaw dropped, and Martinez took his hand and closed it slowly. Mr. Smith did not know all the players and would never have thought of him as one.

Martinez moved closer to the vid, "All going as planned?" The President asked.

"Yes, should be departing *Trinity* in just under two hours."

"I don't need to remind you, Admiral, of the importance of the *Triton System*." The President advised.

Cooper stepped into view, leaning over the President, "I am sure that the Admiral is well aware of our situation and timeline, Sir," The President looked up at him with some annoyance.

Mr. Smith cleared his throat, "Less than a minute."

"Yes, all is going as planned," Martinez replied and then checked his watch, "In thirty-six hours, the *Gamma II* Research station and this system will be mine."

"Mine!" The President corrected him.

Cooper leaned across the desk in front of The President again and turned off the vid.

"Get me *the Roosevelt*," Martinez ordered.

Mr. Smith tapped again, the screen melted again and this time to the bridge of *the Roosevelt* appeared, a short dumpy older man, in his late sixties, with thick gray hair, looking too old for Command, in a white jumpsuit, and not his best color, he sat up quickly, "Admiral?"

"All is going as planned, we'll be on *Gamma II* in less than thirty-six hours, I need you in orbit then, and keep jamming this sector, no one should be able to contact either *the Sol* or *Andromeda Systems*."

"Yes, Sir. And I should inform you, that Admiral Wainwright has been looking into you and why *Gamma II* has gone dark. He sent *the Roanoke.*"

Martinez rubbed his hands together and clapped in delight, "Good, even better than I hoped. No matter, it won't be enough for Bowers, the more the merrier."

Turning back to Mr. Smith, he swiped his hand under his chin from left to right. Mr. Smith tapped a single button, and the vid screen went black, "and all the pieces are coming together nicely." Martinez walked out.

This was unusual to Mr. Smith, as he watched him leave; he had never seen the man this pleased before.

Martinez stepped up to Engineering, and two large, oversized mercenaries stood guard just outside on either side with vacuum rifles. He stopped, and looked to the one on his right, a burly dark-skinned Samoan man, the same man he met on *the Gore*, years earlier, and then to the left, a larger Asian man. They looked down at him since they tower a bit over him in height and back up at each other, and then as if an afterthought, they came to attention. He brushed the dark-skinned man's shoulder, as if he had some dirt, smiled, and then entered Engineering.

Ms. Green was at the console on the upper deck working, with a smaller screen.

"And how are *we* doing, Ms. Green?"

Without looking up, "Good, just finished the shutdown program for one of the power cores. I should be done in about fifteen minutes, and then I can pull one."

"Excellent."

Both look up, hearing the door open. Mr. Jones entered and stopped next to him, "There is something you need to see, Sir?"

Martinez looked at him sideways. He knew this Brut was unable to complete the easiest of tasks and was not happy with how he had been treating his daughter. He looked back over at Ms. Green, and then back at him, "What?"

"Have to show you, Sir," He turned and left.

The two entered the conference room, Mr. Jones continued to the far end of the room and sat. Martinez stopped short, just inside, and scanned it over quickly, "I see nothing here."

"I heard you hired a new guy as your second, and he is on his way with the second squad."

"Yes,"

He slammed the palm of his right hand down on the table and then pointed at Martinez, "You assured me, I was your right-hand man!"

Martinez surveyed the room, again, pulled a small vacuum pistol from under his jacket, from within his waistband, and fired. A single beam of white light traveled across the room, slamming dead center into Mr. Jones's forehead, between his eyes. Mr. Jones's head jerked back; blood sprayed the wall behind him. His body slumped over, hitting the table with a loud thud, "Your first mistake was flirting with my daughter, asshole."

Mr. Smith over the COM, "Sir, the system registered a blast, in sector five."

"Yes, there is a tiny mess in the conference room, please have someone take care of it. . . immediately."

Ms. Green was standing along the back wall in Engineering working out one of the housing units, which was embedded in the wall, and pulled one of the power cores out. It was about two meters tall, by two meters wide squared by three meters deep, a square black case, with a clear glass door front. She pulled it with a quick jerking motion and as gently as possible, it slipped out of her hands, and fell to the floor, with a hard thud, it weighed over a hundred kilograms. She stepped back, and snapped her fingers to someone behind her, "Cargo bay one, now."

The Samoan man stepped up, laid his vacuum rifle on the console, stepped around Green, picked up the core with no fuss as if it had no weight, and carried it past her; she turned and picked up his vacuum rifle, and followed him out.

Martinez, now back in Command, and alone as Cooper appeared on the screen from his office on Capitol Hill, late afternoon on Earth.

"Something wrong, Miguel?"

"You alone?"

"Yes,"

"I found a file disk here; it laid out our entire plan for *Andromeda* and the new experimental weapons."

"Meaning?"

"Estúpido," Martinez yelled, "You're not listening! Someone has leaked out our plans for *Gamma II* and *Andromeda*."

Cooper looked at him with a very confused look, "Who?"

"If I knew that, you think I would be talking to you."

"What are you going to do?"

Martinez closed the channel, "Why I ever choose to work with him. . ."

The console beeped, "Permission to land?" a male voice asked.

"Cargo bay two."

The bay started depressurizing as the whistling sound started. Red lights flooded the bay, as the air pressure vacated. Martinez and Ms. Green were standing in an adjacent room, looking through the window into the bay. The large, oversized door at the rear swung out and down onto the lunar surface; with some dust kicking up. A medium-sized twenty-crew shuttle slowly glided into the bay with a green running light under it and maneuvered slowly and rested with gentle ease onto the deck. Martinez sees two men sitting in the forward compartment.

The large, oversized door rose slowly up and closed; the whistling began again as the air returned to the bay. The red lights stopped, and Ms. Green tapped a few buttons on the console below the window and they exited the outer room, walked around the corner, and into the shuttle bay.

The rear door of the shuttle rises, and two men exit, one African American, and one Hispanic, the Hispanic man has a goatee, and both come around the shuttle. Ms. Green walked a few steps ahead of Martinez, and turned back with her hand out, "May I introduce Mr. Pink and Mr. Red." Mr. Red is dressed as a miner, with a red nylon jacket, and Mr. Pink is in a black jumpsuit like most of the mercenaries.

"Team aboard?" Martinez asked.

"Si, Almirante," Mr. Red replied.

"Follow me, Mr. Red." Martinez turned and left. Ms. Green and Mr. Red followed. Mr. Pink returned to the shuttle.

Martinez, Ms. Green, and Mr. Red enter the conference room. The blood was gone from the wall. Ms. Green hugged Mr. Red tightly. Martinez placed his hands on each of their shoulders, and they looked back at him, "Mi Familia! Finally, my whole family again."

"Sí, Papi," Mr. Red answered.

Martinez stepped back and reached inside his jacket, pulled out a small thin white plastic card, and offered it to Mr. Red, "Coordinates and schedule, when to land, and not be detected by *Gamma II.*"

Mr. Red took the card and kissed his Sister on her cheek and hurried out.

"I have not seen Mr. Jones lately?" Ms. Green asked.

"I fired him," and with that simple remark and knowing her Father, she understood.

* * *

MARS

Admiral Wainwright waited in Senator Macomb's library, milking a glass of bourbon. He was becoming very impatient. Finally, the doors rolled open, "Please follow me, Sir?" the butler asked and turned back. Admiral Wainwright followed him out and off to the right, through a large opening in the wall, into the dining room. In a large area, silk drapes hung on the two windows on the wall to his left, tied in the middle, red drapes, covered with white silk curtains. Another window sat at the far end of the room behind Senator Macomb, who was at the head of the table. Sitting at the far end of a long dining table with twelve high back chairs, mahogany, each carved with an old flag of the Confederate States of America, and there was a larger flag of the Confederate States of America on the wall to his right in a glass and brass case.

I cannot stand him, but I must work with this idiot, Admiral Wainwright thought, as he looked over the grandiose style of this man. A large eight-pronged glass chandelier hung from the ceiling, with three four-pronged candelabras resting on a white tablecloth.

Senator Macomb was wearing a black tuxedo, and holding a long-stemmed black filter for his cigarette, from a bygone era, with three others around him. A female Senator, from Earth in a silky white ball gown, gray hair, and pearl necklace, a very high-class lady, and a larger man from the southern colonies of Mars, bald and wearing a black tuxedo, similar to that of Macomb's. The third man he knew, Rear Admiral Fitzsimmons, both men were wearing their dress uniforms, Navy blue uniforms, coat and slacks, white dress shirts, blue ties, white gloves, and sabers at their sides, Fitzsimmons, was also holding his cigar at his side.

"Admiral," Fitzsimmons said, stood, and came to attention.

Macomb strolled around the long table and passed by the two Senators, "No need for formalities, gentlemen," Admiral Wainwright waved at Fitzsimmons, and he sat. "And you already know the Admiral, may I also present Senators Michaels and Drumwell," first toward the man and then the lady, and sat back down himself.

"We don't have time for parties, Max!"

Shocked, "We always have time for parties, Jack, ol' boy," placing his left hand on his chest and sucking his long cigarette holder.

Admiral Wainwright also sat, looking over the party guest, nodding at Fitzsimmons, who was now puffing on his cigar, which really irritated him. Begrudgingly, Fitzsimmons took it out and looked around where to put it, almost comically. Then the butler stepped up and put his white-gloved hand out, impatiently. Fitzsimmons placed it in his hand, and walked back to the open archway, where he waited, and tossed it into a metal canister.

"I'll be wanting that back when I leave," Fitzsimmons said as he watched it fall into the metal canister, frowning.

Admiral Wainwright grunted. Fitzsimmons sat back. "You said, Bowers was alive and on *Gamma II?* I have also learned Martinez is there, what else can you tell me?

"The Admiral here has learned of a conspiracy at the White House, with the President and Senator Cooper," Macomb explained, pointing at Fitzsimmons.

"Yes, the President, Senator Cooper of Earth, and Martinez are planning a coup, using all the resources they had obtained from their sources and items they have acquired from the *Andromeda Galaxy*, for a staging point on *Gamma II* for a notorious reason in the *Andromeda Galaxy*," Fitzsimmons explained.

It was coming together now, and he was finally gaining answers, "I have already sent *the Roanoke* to find out why they have gone dark, and help them if needed, and I have two operatives in Martinez's group for recon and information gathering," he explained. He looked at Fitzsimmons, who nodded, and understood, "I also will be departing in the morning with a detachment of Marines for *Gamma II*. How will you handle the coup here?" looking at Macomb and then his guests.

"With the help of Fitzsimmons, by your order, being the ranking officer on Mars, he will arrest Orrin and the President at the summit, and I will present the necessary documents to the Vice President for the impeachment of President Tran, which my colleagues and I have acquired."

"We had learned a few months back, that the President was moving funds from relief efforts on Earth to his private accounts, and specialty troops to private bases on *IO* and *Orion six*," Ms. Drumwell added.

"And from relief funds from Earth earmarked for Mars, also a few items Martinez acquired in the *Andromeda Galaxy* a few years back when Bowers was presumed dead, which were locked away here on Mars," Michaels concluded.

It all seemed good to Admiral Wainwright; he may have the upper hand over Martinez this time, "If you can stop them, here on Mars and I on *Gamma II*, we may not have a coup, and might stop him once and for all."

"All seems in order, I do hope you enjoy your holiday on *Gamma II*, Jack," Macomb replied.

As Admiral Wainwright and Fitzsimmons stormed out, Fitzsimmons stopped and picked up his cigar from the metal canister, shook it some, puffed a few times, and was pleased it was still lit. The butler rolled his eyes.

"More champagne, Rochester?" Macomb called out with his glass up, "Now, it's a party."

* * *

THE GORGE

The hot afternoon blistering Sun shined down through a single large gorge, cut out of a canyon on *Gamma II,* Schmitt's Gorge named for Harrison Schmitt, a Geologist, and one of the last men to step foot on the moon, and a true physical scientist and Geologist to study it, in the twentieth century. The gorge was half the size of Earth's Grand Canyon, but this station was positioned right in one of the smaller alcoves and could be seen from orbit.

Two shuttles sat on the canyon floor with both cargo doors facing the station, as if carved out of the rock face, with an identical *Gamma* station inside, Mercenaries and Miners unloaded crates and other cargo.

Ms. Green, was now in Engineering, holding a small flashlight, the only source of light in the room, between her teeth, and then slammed the power core into one of the three empty slots. The dark-haired man and red-haired man who were loading the shuttle on *Trinity* were helping, each clamping two red bars on each side, which she had unclamped on the moon base, as she held it in place. She opened the glass panel, pressed, and held two large flat red buttons simultaneously, they clicked, lit up, and the front panel lights came on. The lights in Engineering flashed a couple of times, and then came on; they heard loud snapping sounds as breakers activated throughout the station.

Martinez clapped from behind her, down the ramp on the main floor behind the console. She turned around and saw him smiling. Martinez tapped the console, "Mr. Smith, you may proceed to Command and begin, I will be there shortly," he waved the two men off, "please find out if we have any little friends, Ms. Green?"

Martinez entered Command as Mr. Smith sat at the main console, he had a small screen out again, with different connecting cables that were attached to the console, and was bringing the rest of the systems online, "How long?"

"Should be online, in thirty minutes," Mr. Smith advised.

"Nice, meet me in the conference room in one hour."

Mr. Red, Mr. Smith, and Ms. Green were waiting, as Martinez entered and shifted to the far end of the conference table, "Now, I can tell you the complete plan and why we are here, Mr. Smith, how long before *the Roosevelt* arrives?"

"Ten hours," Mr. Smith answered.

"Our glorious President wishes to have this planet for a Military base, a staging point for *Andromeda*. . . and I have unfinished business to attend to. However, there is one obstacle in my way, the *Gamma II* crew. There is a plan in the works, to remove them, if that does not work, that is why we are all here," as he looked at Mr. Red.

"Why doesn't the President or you just reassign them?" Mr. Smith asked.

Martinez shot a look right through him coldly, leaning a bit forward, and reaching behind his back.

Ms. Green interrupted, "I did not see any Environmental suits here, and we did not bring any with us, if it takes longer than ten days, how do we handle the carbon dioxide period?"

Martinez laughed out loud, "That was a fucking lie—I thought of----Professor Ranko documented, and Senator Cooper made sure it was believed. We have all the time in the world. Keep telling a lie long enough and it will become the truth."

"And you will inform *the Roosevelt*, once it arrives, also?" Mr. Smith asked.

"Yes," Martinez said with disgust in his voice, "and now excuse me. I now have to send a private communication."

Senator Cooper and the Captain of *the Roosevelt* appeared on a split screen in Command, "Well?" Cooper asked.

"All set here; my people are aware of the plan wanted by the President."

"I will be there in less than ten hours, but we have a little less than ten days until the atmosphere changes," The Captain of *the Roosevelt* stated. Cooper burst out laughing, and the Captain looked confused.

"My dear Captain, I can assure you, there is no carbon dioxide issue, it was a lie I planted years ago to make sure I, Senator Cooper, and a few others, could work in private, however. With the return of Commander Bowers, I know he will never believe it, and that is just too bad for him," Martinez said.

"All right then, no worries," said the Captain of *the Roosevelt*.

Cooper cut in, "I leave it in your hands, Miguel."

Martinez tapped the console. Both screens went black, and then the screen melted back to a window, with a view of the canyon wall.

Two mercenaries, young men, just boys, were walking along the cliff above the station, on patrol, and then started down a small path, cut out of the rock, hiking back down to the canyon floor. The taller one of the two in front, an African American, slipped and slid a good three meters down, spinning many times, and landing face-first, hard into the canyon floor. The other man, with blonde hair, ran after him, jumped ahead of his companion, and checked his pulse; he was dead. As he turned and stood, gaining his balance against the canyon wall, he saw the dirt slowly dropping, and carving something out of the wall.

He fell back in shock into Mr. Red's arms, spun around, and started rambling.

Mr. Red smacked him, "What are you doing, idiot!" and let him drop to the ground, and the boy just pointed at the wall. Mr. Red looked it over, "AWAKE," carved into the wall. He stooped down for a better look, "Who did this?"

The young boy was still shaking, and just pointed at the wall, "It did, it did."

Mr. Red slapped him again, "Mister, who did that?" pointing back at the wall.

"The wall!" the boy kept repeating.

"Eighty percent of the station is online," Mr. Smith advised.

"Good, the jammer still up?" Martinez asked.

"Yes,"

"Can we connect to *Gamma II?*"

"Yes, if you want the computer's voice online?"

"No,"

"Mr. White, Mr. Red needs you, he has found something you need to personally see, a new problem," Ms. Green said, entering Command.

She and Martinez stepped out. Mr. Smith waited for the door to close completely, then removed a small cylinder from his jacket pocket and tapped the top, "Lone wolf to Phoenix, over."

CHAPTER EIGHT

SEARCH AND DESTROY

MACPHERSON AWOKE, with a pounding headache, shifted around lowly in the small area. It was dark and cold, and there was a musty stench in the air, she coughed, and moved her hands around to find her flashlight. She reached out, felt something, and jumped back, reached out again. It was Swanson, lying beside her, "Theresa!" But no response. She shook her, but Swanson just laid there, then checked her pulse.

She heard rocks sliding over rocks, as a doorway opened, and then a light shined in. The light shined through in waves; she thought the waves could only be from torches in the other room, she stood up slowly, still dizzy, and looked up but only saw darkness, except for the light from the other room. Twisted around slowly looking the room over, just stone and the single doorway, no carvings, or writings.

Reaching down she heard Swanson moan and saw her shifting, "Theresa, you all right?"

Rubbing her head slowly, and felt the gash over her right eye, "Yes, Ma'am, I think so." Swanson stood with Macpherson's help, "Where are we?"

"Your guess is as good as mine," Macpherson answered.

Swanson looked up seeing the light coming in, "We were in Environmental Control, and then it felt like an elevator dropped."

"Somehow we must have been transported here."

"Then Bowers was right, there is ancient technology, here," Swanson said.

"But why after ten years? Martinez was here six years ago, and we've been here about a year."

"The force field around the Pyramid!" she remembered the conversation the team had in the conference room when Bowers explained his first visit to the Pyramid.

"What?" Macpherson said, still looking over the room.

"Commander Bowers stated he touched the force field and it dropped, and then the Alien ship launched. Maybe his touch woke up whatever has been messing with us, and launched the ship," Swanson explained, "maybe whatever was here is now linked to Bowers."

"It did attack Bowers first, shortly after his return and our return from Waterman Crater," Macpherson explained, "We were near the Pyramid too when the storm hit, maybe it was not a storm as we know it."

A loud howling shriek as if a wounded animal cried out from the other room.

Macpherson stepped slowly through the doorway cut out of the wall. Swanson followed, seeing the torches on the walls, as she had thought they could only be illuminating the room. On the farthest wall was an oversized black marble Throne. The chair sat atop a platform with three steps, which looked as if carved out of the wall and was shaped like a skull, and two skulls for the armrests.

Coming up from the back and arching over the chair are a dozen arrows facing forward. They continued up and around the Throne, walking around it, it was not at the far wall but in the center of the room. They found behind the massive Throne an oversized chest as if carved out of the wall and floor, over five meters long, four meters wide, and three meters deep. One side had a chunk removed as if blasted out from the inside, and debris all around the floor, "A large sarcophagus," Macpherson commented.

"Like in Egypt?"

"Yes, but older, I think the stonework predates them."

Swanson ran her hand over it. "Feels like metal."

Macpherson ran her hand over it too, "It's also cool to the touch."

"Is this stone or metal?"

Macpherson shifted behind the sarcophagus and ran her hand over the wall, "It's cool too. How can that be?"

A high-pitched tone started and rose in volume, each covering their ears, yelling but could not hear the other, holding their ears, they collapsed and passed out.

The tone ceased.

Hitchcock sat on a stone ledge across the room from Adams, who was slamming his whole body into a wooden door, an opening that was cut out of the stonewall, "How many times does it take before you give up, Earl?"

He slammed himself against the door again, "Till it opens or breaks."

Hitchcock stood, "We're stuck here."

"Where is here? The last thing I remember was you coming into Engineering and then poof, we're here," Adams tossed his arms up, "But how? You're the scientist, I am just an engineer."

"If you give me a minute, I may be able to figure it out," Hitchcock said as he placed his hand on his shoulder.

"Good luck," Adams said, sitting back on the ledge.

Hitchcock slowly ran his hand over the wall on both sides, then heard a click, the door swung out, and a bright flickering light shined in.

"How the fuck. . ." Adams said.

"I was thinking, while you were knocking on the door, how we got here, we must have been transported, somehow. If we were transported, then maybe some ancient technology," Adams stared at him with a questioning look, "Yes, I read Bowers's report, maybe he was right, ancient technology," Hitchcock explained.

"Go figure,"

A loud howling shriek as if a wounded animal cried out from the other room.

Hitchcock and Adams move from the confined room into the next and immediately encounter a chamber with a long descending staircase. Hitchcock took one of the many torches off the wall, and tossed it down, landing down about ten steps. They looked at each other; then each grabbed a torch and descended the staircase. Slowly one step at a time, each reaching the bottom as more torches quickly lit up, illuminating the room, and Adams looked back at Hitchcock, "How?"

"Air movement," Hitchcock replied.

Adams just shook his head, he did not want to get him started, and then he noticed a ledge on the far wall, "Slow down, Earl," Hitchcock yelled, taking off after him, as he now noticed the ledge, seeing what looked like grooves and buttons. Adams ran his hand over it, moving the dust away. He pressed on, and the table lit up, they heard a whistling sound, a green light surrounded them, and they vanished.

Bowers said on the edge of a bed, and leaned forward, letting out a heavy sigh; he was tired and started to undo the Velcro straps on his boots, the door chimes, "Enter."

Walker-Swanson entered with a look of disgust. She never wanted him here, but now she needed his help. Bowers stood.

"Sir?"

"Is there a problem, Lieutenant?"

She hesitated, "The Captain is now missing, and with Mr. Hitchcock also missing, by General Order thirty-two, I am required to inform the senior most officer of our current situation, which is . . . you," and then she let out a long sigh.

"What you mean, is missing?"

"Mitchell and I had finished repairs in Engineering, and I returned to Command, and *Gamma* informed me she was missing."

"Last time I saw her, *Gamma* stated she was needed in Environmental Control. *Gamma*, please confirm?"

"I have no log entry of that, Commander Bowers," *Gamma* replied.

"We were both in Command; we were watching the tape of Hitchcock, and noticing his eyes, and then you called her to Environmental Control."

"My logs do not reflect that, Sir."

"What was her last reported location?" Bowers ordered.

"Captain Macpherson is in the conference room," *Gamma* answered. Walker-Swanson shook her head, no.

"You just reported she was not in the station."

"Yes, Sir."

"Which is it, is she missing, *Gamma*, or is she in the conference room?"

"Yes, Sir."

"Now you know why I am here, Sir," Walker-Swanson said.

Bowers lets out a heavy sigh, "*Gamma,* diagnostic mode, Alpha one command, lockdown, now!" Bowers ordered. The screen on his console came to life, data files began to scroll up, and the station schematics displayed as if searching for something, "*Gamma* has more than corrupted files. You, Mitchell, and Calvin start a physical search of the station, starting with Environmental Control, then the bays, and I will check Command, and advise the Doctor."

She nodded and left quickly.

Bowers found the Doctor and Swanson cleaning the medical bay, "Doctor, have you seen the Captain?"

"Not since the meeting, when you and her left, quickly."

"We went to Engineering, then to Command, she was called to Environmental Control, but *Gamma* has no record of it, shows her in the conference room, and missing."

"Then, that is why the station is on lockdown," the Doctor said.

Bowers turned to Swanson, "Can you excuse us Ensign," She left but watched him closely.

"Doctor, I have to ask you to do something, no one should."

The Doctor looked at him as a Father looks when a child was asking permission to do something, he knew was wrong, "Daniel?"

"Check her logs for anything out of the ordinary."

The Doctor sighed and sat, "Dan, you know what you're asking me?"

"Yes, but I need to know everything she was thinking, just in case."

The Doctor understood; he needed to know what she was thinking as her last thoughts if she was dead.

Swanson continued down the corridor, paused at the four-way junction, and looked back, thinking someone was following her. Turned and continued down the path to her left, her shadow morphed into the shadow of the cloaked figure, and continued down the hallway, with an echoing laugh.

A loud howling shriek as if a wounded animal cried out.

Down the opposite hallway, an explosion rocks the station, debris flies into the other hallways, and alarms sound off. Mitchell ran to his right in the direction of the explosion.

Bowers and Walker-Swanson followed, as they entered the cargo bay, they found the Copernicus destroyed and taking most of the outer bay door with it, and the window into the adjacent room.

Mitchell knocked the remaining glass out of the way, and jumped through, he moved the debris around, and found no one there, "Clear!"

Bowers walked past most of the debris and stepped outside through what was left of the bay door, scanned the area, and across the desert, seeing a single small flash of light amongst the rocks, a few kilometers across the desert.

"See something, Sir?" Walker-Swanson asked.

"No," he walked back in, surveying the damage, and stooped down, moved a large piece of the bulkhead of the shuttle, not hearing her, passed it off, and moved more of the debris around.

Mitchell joined them with what looked like a timing device, number pad, circuit board, and wires hanging off, "Found this where the pilot's chair used to be."

All looked back where the pilot's chair was, and saw Calvin, now standing there and looking down, and then back up at them with a sickening look on his face, realizing that was where he died.

Bowers took the device, "Continue the search." Mitchell nodded and turned, patting Calvin on the shoulder, who was now shaking his head, and they walked out.

"Think this was your cloaked figure?" Walker-Swanson asked.

"No, unless he can use our technology, this is resistance tech, like the device Doc found in Adams."

"Chief Adams?"

"Not his style, and I don't think we are alone anymore," Bowers answered he remembered *Gamma* stated, Ranko said we are not alone in this world or the quadrant of space and then looked back over her shoulder, she turned, and looked where he was looking, "and I don't mean the cloaked figure."

From far across the desert, a man was looking through binoculars. He lowered them. It was Martinez, and he was smiling, "Check." From what he just watched and knows Bowers does not realize, that he is on the planet.

"Phase one, done?" Mr. Red asked, standing next to him.

"Yes, that will keep them busy. Now, show me what you found?"

Both walked down a few rocky steps, into the canyon behind them, "You told me Bowers always beat you at chess?"

"Not this time."

Mr. Pink was leaning over, taking a better look at the carving in the wall, AWAKE, and was running his fingers in and around the crevasse as they joined him.

"What did you find, Mr. Pink?" Martinez asked.

Mr. Pink turns around, "Not I, Sir. The boy over there," pointing at the young boy near the large cargo bay, with two medical technicians in miner's outfits, he was sipping water and they were trying to calm him.

Martinez looked in the direction Mr. Pink was pointing. Mr. Pink stepped aside so they could see the carving better, "I found the boy staring at this, with his partner dead after falling here from the path up there," Mr. Red stated pointing at the wall, then up at the high cliff.

Martinez leaned forward and looked it over, "Looks recent, someone playing a joke."

"The boy stated, as he was resting against the wall after checking his partner out, and it just appeared," Mr. Red said.

Martinez not believing this, took out his pocketknife, flipped it open, and cut into the wall, other than some flakes, the stone was too hard to break with just his pocketknife, "What tools do we have that could do this?"

"Nothing that accurate, Sir, this was done with a precession laser," Mr. Pink replied.

Martinez quickly walked over to the cargo bay. Mr. Red followed, and he stooped down in front of the boy, "Now tell me the truth, son. How did you do that?" Martinez asked.

The young boy looked at him oddly and started talking fast, "It did it, it did it," he kept repeating himself.

Martinez stood and looked back at Mr. Red, with his back to the young boy, "We don't need sniveling kids here, Mr. Red," as he crossed his right hand under his chin from the left. Mr. Red nodded. Martinez stooped back down and patted the young boy on his head, "It will be okay, son. Take it easy," and walked off.

Mr. Red waved the two medical technicians off, and helped the boy up, "Come with me," and waved him forward, "Let us look at that again."

Ms. Green was checking over a report in the cargo bay across from the entrance and flipped a page over, with another female technician in a miner's outfit next to her. A pistol shot rang out, the female miner jumped, and Ms. Green looked up, then back to the file.

A green light flashed, and Hitchcock and Adams appeared face down and unconscious in the Throne room. Swanson and Macpherson were still lying unconscious near the sarcophagus, behind the Throne. The Cloaked figure entered from the adjacent room, where Macpherson and Swanson started, walked around slowly, and looked over Adams and Hitchcock. Then moved behind the Throne, his eyes glowed red under his cloak, he stoops down, and waved his arm over Macpherson's body, she slowly faded away, then it shifted to Swanson, and waved its arm again, the cut on her forehead disappeared, and then she faded away also. He stood up quickly and spun around, returning to the front of the Throne, and sat, crossing his hands in front of his chest, resting his elbows on the armrests, twisted his head around, letting out a loud howling shriek as if a wounded animal cried out, and looked down at them with his red eyes glowing brighter.

Hitchcock steered. Adams jumped up, "What the fuck!"

"I am Mishophar! [Mis'o'far] Why are you on my planet?" It yelled with a low gravelly voice, booming loudly, resonating off the walls.

"What the fuck!" Adams repeated.

Red bolts flash from his hands, and tossed Adams across the room, "Kneel, peasants!" Mishophar [Mis' o' far] commanded, Hitchcock quickly shifted and knelt, with head and eyes down.

Adams stood again, "Go to hell, you mother—"

Bolts again flash from Mishophar's hands, blasting Adams across the room into the wall, vaporizing him.

Still looking over the timing device, Bowers returned to Command and laid it on the console, the screen still running files and the station schematics, he tapped a key on the console, and the screen went black. He looked over the device knowing it was resistance tech, and he had seen it before, Calvin walked in, his jumpsuit covered with oil and gunk, on his face had muddy oil stains, and then Bowers smelled the stench, he turned around and saw Calvin.

Calvin wiped some of the gunk from his eyes, "Sir, sorry to report, Captain Macpherson, Swanson, Hitchcock, and Adams are nowhere in the station."

Remembering, he just saw Swanson in the medical bay, "And whose idea was it for you to crawl through the recycling slug pump?" Already knowing the answer.

"May I go clean up, Sir?"

"Yes," Bowers replied as Walker-Swanson entered and Calvin left.

"You had him crawl through the recycling slug pump?"

"The screen showed something or someone in there, I am a senior officer," she answered with a slight smile.

"Sorry about Swanson, we'll find her, and the others."

Shock boils up on her face, not knowing her wife was missing, "What!"

"I thought you knew. Calvin reported her missing too."

"Should have told me first," Tears started, but she held her composure.

"Yes," Bowers said, standing there, "We'll find them all."

She left quickly, nearly hitting Mabuto, as he was coming in.

"Sorry, Dan, I did not find anything worth reporting."

"You heard about Swanson?"

"Yes, Thomas advised me. Half the team gone, what is your plan, now?"

Bowers looked out the window, out over the desert, "I was planning on returning to the Pyramid, but now with most of the crew missing, and the blast, mine is not the priority anymore."

Mr. Smith was still working in Command, as Ms. Green entered and looked over the room, seeing five large metal cases. The center console's panel opened and held in place with a single metal bar on the right side, and he was working inside. Cables hanging out from the console, tool kits on the floor, one of the cases had cables hanging out and a few system boards on top. She walked around in front of the console.

"How's it going?" She said quickly. He jumped, hitting his head on the panel and she giggled.

"Very funny, I'm almost done, and you have to love how man has become *so* lazy, these off-world sites and most space vessels are built the same: the panels, windows ugly brown carpet, systems boards, and cables," He stated pointing at the objects in the room. "As soon as Mr. White gives the word, we can proceed, and I was even able to delete the damn female voice for the station's computer."

"I will let Mr. White know," Ms. Green said leaving.

A single chirp sounded, and Mr. Smith pulled out the small cylinder from his pocket, "Lone wolf, over."

"Status updates, Phoenix, over," over the link, Admiral Wainwright asked.

"Finishing now, over."

"Good, over." A single chirp again, and Mr. Smith put the link away.

Martinez entered, "So, how much longer?"

"Twenty minutes. Need to clean up here, and then we'll be on schedule with *the Roosevelt*," He answered as he closed the panel, and locked it back into place.

"Good, notify me when Captain Cooke and his team land with the final equipment," Martinez ordered looking around then left.

Mr. Smith took a small metal elongated box, from the open case, and opened it, a black panel with 00:00:00, displayed, and with wires hanging off. Almost like the one Bowers found after the explosion. Three buttons, one red, one green, and one blue, near the numbers. He pressed the blue button and held it, and the numbers changed to 00:20:00. He released the blue button and they returned to 00:00:00. He pulled out a small black cylinder, with a thin red cover, flipped it up, a metal switch, and put the red cover back down.

Placed it in his lower pocket, placed the timer under the center console, and moved two of the large metal cases that were not open, slowly, and gently near the front console on each side of the room.

CHAPTER NINE

UNDER THE PYRAMID

CALVIN HAD FINISHED HIS SHOWER, DRESSED, and then started to leave his quarters, but stopped, he sat back on his bed and debated between heading off to bed or reporting to Bowers for his next assignment. Bowers was not officially his Commanding officer but was the ranking officer on station at present and had treated him with more respect than any other Commander, he had been with since serving in the Earth Alliance, including Macpherson, but he chose to sleep. He was not sure if it was swimming through the recycling slug pump for an hour or collecting the debris from the shuttle with Mitchell that wore him out the most, or the fact that he was dead for three days. Dying can take a lot out of a person.

He was in deep thought with his conundrum that he did not see Mishophar [Mes'o'far] standing outside his large bay window off to his right. The tall looming figure's red eyes flashed against the night. He made his way back up the bed. Mishophar's eyes flash twice. A red light cascaded over him, and he was gone, Mishophar [Mes'o'far] let out an echoing laugh and then vanished with a crack of thunder.

Walker-Swanson found Bowers still working at the center console in Command, "It's late, Sir, we're all tired and can continue the search in the morning," he did not hear her at first, she placed her hand on his shoulder, and he turned around, and saw the red light cascade over her as she vanished, and he heard Mishophar's [Mes'o'far] echoing laugh.

Two more were missing, this was not a game, and it confirmed he had awoken something, something more powerful than he could ever imagine. It was taking his people, his only friends after ten years, some good, some bad, but his friends. It was down to him and whatever he had awoken. The laugh echoed through his mind, goading him.

Bowers looked up as the door slid open, seeing Mishophar standing there, "I warned you, Commander, and now they will pay the ultimate price!" Bowers vanished, the red light that had cascaded over the others, now washed over him, as Mishophar's echoing laugh resonated through the station, and he was gone, the console beeped. "Please restate inquiry?" *Gamma* asked.

Hitchcock was still kneeling with head and eyes down, waiting, but from where he was, he did not know Mishophar [Mes'o'far] was no longer there, he slowly raised his head but kept his eyes down, and then he saw the empty Throne, and let out a heavy sigh, stood, and looked around, only to see the wall with a black burnt shadow of Adams, "I am so sorry Earl," and he quickly grabbed a torch off the wall, and ran into the adjacent room, and found nothing, and returned. He looked over the Throne slowly, looking closer at each skull, and ran his hands over each, finding an indentation on top of the right one. He hesitated for a moment and then slowly pressed it, the wall to the left of the Throne, behind him rose, and he heard rocks sliding over rocks, turned fast, and found a large dark room, only heard clicks and beeps from machinery or computers.

A few lights near the back started to glow and he saw two vertical elongated tubes, near the back wall, he could see two figures in each, and he recognized them, Macpherson, and Swanson. He ran up fast, more lights came on, and he heard the rolling rocks again, turned back, and watched as the wall came down.

Bowers coughed. He was face down in the dirt. It was morning now, he slowly got up onto his knees, then hiked himself up, and saw he was on the rim of the massive gorge, which the Ancient ship had left, after launching ten years ago, and looked over the edge, and saw nothing; it was still massive as he remembered. He turned fast, looked up, and saw the Ram's head on the Pyramid; he was back where it all started.

Moved closer, with an outstretched hand, feeling for the force field, but it was not there. He reached the top of a set of descending stone stairs and with instinct, he reached to his belt for a flashlight but found nothing.

He started down slowly, each step, one at a time, counting about ten, reached the bottom, the ceiling above him blocking most of the Sunlight but even in the dark, he could make out an oversized door. Five meters wide, three meters tall, and in the middle, an image of the *Sol System* was carved out, but there were two planets where Earth sat.

Remembering back to his Mother's teachings, *there is always a way in Danny, every door has a lock and key, but it is never obvious.* He remembered from his childhood when his Mother unlocked *her* Pyramid, back on Earth. He ran his right hand over the wall and images; he felt a grove running from one of the twin planets over to the nearby fifth planet. He let out a heavy sigh and slowly with a fingertip pushed one of the twins along the grove to the other planet's position and heard a clicking noise and heard it lock it into place. He stepped back as the wall of the entrance started to rise, dust and dirt fell from the area between the entrance and the stone structure.

Hitchcock walked up to the two pods, the brightest lights in the room, and from what he could tell this was not Ancient technology, it was current, current technology from a hundred years ago, and looked over the panels to his side. *How could there be current technology, here in an Ancient Pyramid, over a thousand millennia old, older than dirt itself,* he thought. He reached up and pressed a red button on the back panel behind one of the pods, the pod holding Macpherson brightened a bit more and dimmed out, she took in a deep breath, and the pod rose into the ceiling, she dropped to the floor, and he tried to catch her.

She coughed, and saw him on top of her, "You can get off of me now." He stood quickly and helped her up, "Where are we? Last I remember I was in a Throne room, and there was this high-pitched sound."

"That room is behind that wall," he pointed at the far wall, "and I am not sure about this room, but I think we are in the Pyramid."

"How did you—we get here?"

"That I do not know, Adams and I were trapped, I found the way to open the wooden door in the stone cell we were trapped in, after I stepped into Engineering. We went down some steps and found an old panel, stone but from how it felt, it was metal. Earl, not thinking as usual, started pressing buttons, and we were transported to the Throne room, and the cloaked figure was sitting on the Throne and called itself Mishophar [Mes'o'far]."

"You saw it, it spoke to you?"

"Whatever it was, it was still under the cloak, and only saw its red eyes glaring, and it told us peasants to kneel before him. Adams refused, but something told me too."

Your cowardice, she told herself, "Then . . ."

"I heard Adams bitching it out, and then I heard something hit the back wall and Adams yelled, after a time I got up, and Adams was gone, he's dead Ma'am. Then I examined the Throne and found this room, and you two."

"You got me out, can you get her out?"

"Yes, this is one of our old sleeper ships, its control room, from a hundred years ago." He pressed another red button behind the other pod, and it brightened, Swanson took a deep breath, and it slowly rose, she fell, and they caught her.

Swanson coughed, "What happened?"

"We are still learning, seems we're in the Pyramid, and now one of our old sleeper ships," Macpherson said as they helped her into one of the chairs by the console.

Hitchcock looked over the console ran a hand up to a dial and twisted it, the lights came on fully, and they could see the room better, "Yes, it is one of our old sleeper ships," Hitchcock advised them. They see two other pods across the room, near the wall next to the Throne room, but they are empty.

Macpherson noticed a steel door off behind the two additional pods, "This way," and they followed Macpherson and Hitchcock pulled at the wheel of the steel door, taking some effort but finally the wheel turned, and as they opened the door, the air in the next room smelled awful, like death.

The room opened onto an old medical bay, like theirs in *Gamma,* but older. The beds along the back were cots, not raised pads, an old wooden oak desk, older than either of them, with papers scattered over it.

Macpherson started looking over the papers, but they were not giving her any answers. Back along the wall by one of the cots was another steel door. "There," Swanson said. They tried this wheel, and this one moved with ease, and opened onto a stone tunnel,

"Definitely in the pyramid," Macpherson commented.

"But why only part of a ship?" Swanson asked, but Hitchcock and Macpherson had no answers.

"That's a mystery for another time, Ensign. If we all live through this. . ." Macpherson stated.

Hitchcock cut her off with a raised fist and pointed down the hall seeing lights from torches.

Moving slowly and patiently, looking around the corner but seeing nothing but another hallway, with many torches, she took one, "I don't think we should split up," Macpherson advised.

Both nodded and followed her down the new stone hallway, Hitchcock grabbed another torch and brought up the rear.

Macpherson stopped the group with a closed fist, as she noticed something on the floor ahead of them, a body----it was Calvin. She leaned down taking his pulse.

"I'm still alive."

Swanson and the Captain helped him to his feet, "How did you get here?" Swanson asked.

Getting to his feet, supporting himself with the wall, "Not sure, I was climbing into bed one moment, and then feeling fingers on the back of my neck, the next. Where are we?" As he studied his new surroundings and his three companions near him.

"Sorry, those were mind," Macpherson said as she wiggled her fingers, "and we believe inside the Pyramid," Macpherson answered as the floor dropped out from under them.

The room was massive, a kilometer or more high. Not like the long tunnel his Mother found in hers. A huge stone fire pit ignited in the center of the room, illuminating Bowers's new surroundings. Flames from the fire allowed him to see the walls and room better, and he noticed the writings, which he could read Egyptian hieroglyphs. Two million light-years from Earth, and about seven millennia in the past, give or take a millennium, and a perfect text for him to read, but how?

Bowers looked closer. It was not hieroglyphs, it was changing into hieroglyphics from a picture form of heavy dark circular, and zigzagging squared lines, something or someone was reading his mind, or could his mind be translating? His mind was opening, and filling with information, too fast, and he could not understand it all. The new images were just flashes. *A physical download of data,* he thought, as if he were learning several subjects at once.

Egyptian hieroglyphics and Mesopotamian cuneiform writing were the first languages his Mother had taught him before he had studied English and French in school. He studied the walls closely, found the beginning, and read:

> K'Tal, an old and glorious race at its height, controlled over half the known universe, and the four known galaxies around it. They were a militaristic race, conquering and controlling all worlds they encountered, leaving only death and blood in their wake. K'Tal was on the outer arm of a spiral galaxy. Belarus, [B'lar'rus] their Sun, was a small yellow dwarf, surrounded by nine planets. Having two sister planets rotating around each other, and one with a single solitary moon. Cha'tain and K'Tal sat in an orbit of approximately two hundred million kilometers from Belarus [B'lar'rus]. K'Tal was a radiant blue-green jewel, mostly water, with only about thirty-five percent landmass. Cha'tain was a desolate

rock, with little water. K'Tal supported many species. Cha'tain and K'Tal had over fifteen billion people after the colonization of Cha'tain. They had taken this world over one hundred millennia prior and came together as one, but at the same time, depleting over ninety percent of their resources, but only twenty millennia to conquer the four known galaxies. They ripped apart and enslaved worlds, using their resources until they depleted them. Then the K'Tal race came upon a new system. They named it Sol'en, with a small yellow dwarf Sun, similar to theirs, it hovered solitarily in space, encircled by nine worlds, like their own. Five rocky-type worlds near the Sun, one a dead world, with no atmosphere, the second a rocky world, with a carbon-dioxide atmosphere, a third, a vivid blue-green jewel, with five continents, and two polar ice caps, and a single solitary moon hovering around it. The fourth world, half the size of the third, the twin to the third was also a blue-green jewel, with three large continents, and four large oceans, having two small moons encircling it, in really small asteroids. The fifth world was rocky and barren with a very thin atmosphere, smaller than the fourth, with little water, and only a small ice cap near the Southern Pole. Five worlds Mishophar could strip and alter for himself; however, Mishophar fell in love with these worlds. Like his twins, K'Tal and Cha'tain, which encircled each other, he had five worlds, two like his own twins. Besides the remaining four worlds, two large hot-gas giants, one with rings, and two lesser ice worlds, he found the heaven, like Bor [his great-grandfather] knew many millennia before. He named them Vahdowa and Shat'a, which meant "open land" and "endless land." He colonized Vahdowa, on the two largest landmasses, one that sat mostly below the equator but also above, and on the largest continent above the equator, spanning most of the northern hemisphere: each group landing and staying within an area about fifty kilometers north and south. Mishophar returned to K'Tal, after hearing of a coup by his brother, he left Vahdowa as an Outpost in hopes of returning one day but never did. It remained free and untouched for the five hundred thousand colonists, but then after two millennia, a large comet hurling through the solar system slammed into the fifth planet. Demolishing it, leaving behind an asteroid field, which altered the axis of the fourth planet, turning it into a desolate rock in space, positioning it near the location of the old fifth planet, ripping most of its atmosphere off, and leaving a thinner one in its place; the twins were no more. When Mishophar heard of the devastation of his twins, it pained him. He would never return, because his people had rioted and killed the ruling family, shortly after his return, finding a bloody coup that had released a bombardment from space, turning both beautiful worlds to rubble before his eyes and destroyed, by his most trusted Commander, his wife. Now entombed in the royal Pyramid, swearing if anyone stepped foot on his twins again, he would destroy them both once and for all. K'Tal and Cha'tain now long dead, among the endless night sky, two large rocks in space, waiting.

"Mon Dieu [My God], Earth is the Lost Outpost of K'Tal, we are the descendants of the old colony, I should have known. It was not my system, but Belarus' [B'lar'rus] on the door, we have come home."

Bowers yelled louder, "We have come home!"

Hearing rocks rolling over rocks, the ceiling opened, and the bright sunlight shined in. He turned fast feeling a presence, and the fire pit went out, and on the other side of the pit, Mishophar [Mes'o'far] stood.

Bowers sidesteps back toward the entrance slowly, keeping his eyes on the large looming figure, his eyes glowing, and then Bowers darted for the entrance, Mishophar raised his right arm, and the stone entrance closed fast, cutting off his only path out, and as Mishophar dropped his arm, the floor near the entrance dropped out from under, and Mishophar let out a hellish scream that echoed.

Walker-Swanson burst through the surface first, falling back into the water, coughing. It was dark. She tried to stay afloat, and then something else broke through the surface, it was Macpherson and Calvin. She let out a horrifying scream, not knowing what it was or who it was, with her eyes closed. Macpherson grabbed her, "It's okay, it's okay, Kathy, it's me, Bekka." Swanson slowly opened her eyes and saw Macpherson, grabbed her, they jumped as two more broke the surface, Hitchcock, and Swanson, and even in the darkness, Walker-Swanson could hear her wife's cough. She swam over and held her close, Swanson jumped and screamed, then saw it was Walker-Swanson, and held her tight.

Macpherson yelled, "Call out."

"Hitchcock,"

"Calvin,"

"Swansons," Walker-Swanson replied.

They moved closer together as a huge wave crashed down around them, and they heard a loud whistling.

"I don't think we are alone," Hitchcock said, as all were shivering from the freezing water.

"Captain!" Calvin yelled and he pointed. She turned toward his voice. A short way off. there was a fire on what looked like a beach.

"Okay, swim for it!" Macpherson ordered.

"Sure, it's safe?" Hitchcock asked with concern.

"Dry land is better than freezing here and finding out what the hell that was," Macpherson answered.

They swam as fast as they could, the Swansons kept together. They reached the shore and saw a body next to a fire. Macpherson waved the Swansons and Hitchcock off to one side, near the cliff face. She picked up a tree branch that was near the fire. She had not seen any trees on this planet since their arrival, *how could the fire and wood be here?* She thought.

She motioned for Calvin to flank the body to her left, behind the fire, she raised the branch and started to swing, "Wait!" Calvin yelled.

The body rolled over, after hearing Calvin yell, "Bowers, I almost killed you." Macpherson said.

Bowers raised his right hand to block the branch as Macpherson dropped it and dropped to her knees, Hitchcock and the Swansons ran over, realizing it was Bowers.

Bowers laughed, "Good to see you too, Bekka."

Calvin noticed a large piece of meat cooking in the fire and reached for it but pulled back from the heat, Bowers stopped him, "Like the branch and the wood in the fire, there are no animals on this planet, we need to be careful, and we don't know how all this got here," Bowers advised.

"But I'm hungry," Swanson said.

Bowers looked at the group, "I wish I had a screen," he answered, and slowly moved toward the fire, pulled out his pocketknife, which he had in his left pants pocket that he kept from his old flight suit, and opened it. Looked back at Macpherson and the Swansons; they all looked at him with anticipation; Swanson was even licking her lips. Trying not to burn himself, he gently cut a sliver off, stabbed it with his knife, sniffed it, and touched it to his tongue. Chewed some and swallowed, looked around grabbed his throat, fell back, and let out a scream.

Macpherson jumped and then saw his smile, and slapped him, she was not amused.

Bowers moved back to the fire, and giggled, "Tastes like chicken, a bit burned, but all right," he said as he cut more off and tossed them around, and they ate their fill.

After the meal, the Swansons and Calvin slept near the fire, the Swansons holding each other tight.

Hitchcock was back at the beach and looking out over the huge ocean. Wondering about what they had heard, this was a triumph to him, he was stationed here because of his Meteorological skills, but he was an Oceanographer.

After tasting the water, *salty, an ocean,* he told himself.

Macpherson awoke, looked around, and saw Bowers near the cliff face, "How do you think that got here, and that entire Ocean?" she asked as she pointed toward the fire, and then the Ocean.

"Not sure of the meat and fire, but the Ocean. Do you remember the history of Mars?" She nodded, "The first deep survey crew found an Ocean two hundred kilometers under the planet's surface, running most of the area from the north pole to the equator, I believe it to be the same here. I don't remember being in it, but I do have a mouth full of salt water," Bowers explained, "and I'm wondering who dragged me on shore, and left us this meal, and fire."

"We heard a whistling sound, and a wave hit us before we saw the fire," Macpherson stated.

"Maybe a species of dolphin or whale, like they found on Mars, by the deep Ocean explores."

"Life evolved down here?"

"Not sure if it evolved here or on the surface, and came down here for survival, after the destruction above."

"Meaning?" Macpherson asked with a puzzling look.

"Like most of us, we woke up here after being transported. I was outside the Pyramid."

"At least you got back to it like you wanted," Macpherson said giggling trying to offer a joke.

"I found to my shock the force field was still down, and I found at the bottom of the entrance under the Ram's head, the opening and was able to open it. . ."

"A trick your mom taught you, right?" Swanson cuts him off as the rest join.

"Once opened, I found the walls with hieroglyphics."

"Egyptian, right?" Calvin blurted out.

He told them the story of the K'Tal race. how after many eons they controlled this part of the galaxy. Destroying all in their wake, and then finding our system, not as it is now, but exactly as the *Triton System,*

Mars, and Earth were twins, and a fifth rocky planet compared to Mars, where the Asteroid belt is today. How a comet destroyed the fifth planet only confirmed what most scientists believe, and their theories that it was a planet at one time, and Mars shifted near its position.

Of the colony left by Mishophar and his return home to stop a rebellion, how his people destroy this planet from a planetary bombardment and all life. Mishophar's tomb in the Pyramid, and the curse, he will destroy it if anyone ever steps foot on it again.

They all sat there taking it in, "Hard to believe but does answer some historical and scientific questions, we have asked since the dawn of time," Hitchcock added.

"So up there, the planet is dead, but it has continued down here?" Walker-Swanson asked.

"Yes and no. Yes, it did die many eons ago, but after a time, ecosystems restart and rebuild. Professor Ranko told me before I came here. There was a lush world at least twenty years ago, and possibly very habitable, but in less than five years, it has become as it is now. Something happened, maybe once this is all over, Oceanographer Hitchcock and I can figure it out." Hitchcock nodded and Bowers stood, looked up, and yelled, "Mishophar, time for answers!"

A crack of thunder and Bowers vanished.

Martinez peered through his binoculars at *Gamma II* across the plateau, seeing no movement, and the bay door still ripped apart from the blast, "Time to move." He climbed down off the small ledge and into a metal electric jeep, simple in design, just enough to hold the seats, battery pack, and axle. Ms. Green was in the back and Mr. Red was at the wheel; he tossed the binoculars over his shoulder and waved Mr. Red to move out.

Mr. Red drove off, followed by two large electric vehicles, with three wheels on each of their back axles, with the remaining mercenaries aboard. Racing up to the open bay, a handful of mercenaries jumped out of the first vehicle and took up positions on each side. The remaining group ran fast to and secured the station, Mr. Red yelled to hurry them up and waved them on, as he climbed out of the jeep.

Martinez stood outside the bay, taking it all in. Ms. Green places a hand on her Father's shoulder. He smiled at her, and the three entered. His army stormed the station in teams of four, fanning out in all directions, searching room by room, and leaving a man at each door as they moved forward.

Two Mercenaries entered Command, Mitchell was at the far console, the two grabbed him, zip-tied his hands, placed a canvass bag over his head, and dragged him out, "Hey, what is this?"

In the medical bay, Mabuto at the console, four men stormed in, grabbed him, zip-tied his hands, and put a bag on his head, and dragged him out.

Martinez strolled into the conference room with the table pushed back against the far wall. Two chairs sat in the middle, Mitchell and Mabuto were tied to them, and still with the bags on their heads. One of the mercenaries pulled the bag off of Mabuto. His eyes widened as he saw Martinez and his family file in, "What is the meaning of this, Miguel?"

Clapping his hands as he strolled around the room, and looked out the window, and then turned back quickly toward Mabuto, "The meaning of this, where is Bowers? I was told he was here!" Martinez said as he backhanded the Doctor.

Mitchell jumped, but still couldn't move, "Hey!"

"It's all right, Thomas, just do as they want."

"Yes, Thomas, just do as we want," Martinez backhanded the young man, knocking him out, "I am going to ask you one more time, Remy," Martinez said as he pulled the slide back on his old .45 and placed it at Mitchell's head.

The large Samoan man entered, and whispered into Ms. Green's ear, then waited, "Mr. White," she said stopping him, "teams have reported in, there is no one else in the facility."

Martinez yelled, "Betrayed!" and he seemed to go mad, "It was simple—it was a simple plan, simple enough. I'd take this place, kill Bowers, and it was done, but he slipped right out of my hands." Ms. Green looked at her Father as if he had lost his mind. He stopped, seeing the concern on her face, and put his pistol in his waistband, and hurried out, "Keep them here," he ordered, and Ms. Green followed.

They enter Command, and he moves to the far end, "I had him, Pilar. I had him in my hands," Clenching his fists, and then slamming them down on the console, it beeped.

"He may not have gotten far, we have the whole planet under surveillance, and no crafts have left," Ms. Green advised.

He straightened up, composing himself, and looked out the window.

"Computer, location of Commander Bowers?" Pilar asked, but the computer did not respond. She sat, and tapped a few times, "Something was going on here, the computer is in an Alpha one command lockdown," she looked up at him, questioning, not knowing the command.

He turned slowly, "It's an old command code to keep the computer busy when the system was out of control but has not been used in over a couple of decades."

"So, he was here?"

"Yes!" Martinez answered as he tapped his code into the console.

"System ready," *Gamma* answered.

"Location of the Command staff and whereabouts of Commander Bowers?" Pilar asked.

"Working ---- Commander Bowers and staff other than Doctor Mabuto and Technician Mitchell have been transported to the Pyramid on the far side of the planet."

They look at each other, "How?" Martinez demanded.

"No data to account for how, but sensors are reading five life signs deep under the Pyramid, and one in an upper chamber."

They both looked at the sensor map, "That is the chamber Bowers could not read ten years ago," tapping his finger on the sensor map with five blue dots under the Pyramid, he stormed out with Ms. Green following. They returned to the conference room, Mabuto and Mitchell were still tied, and the bag was off Mitchell's head, and he was coming around.

"Computer, repeat initial inquiry!" Martinez ordered.

"Commander Bowers and staff other than Doctor Mabuto and Technician Mitchell have been transported to the Pyramid on the far side of the planet."

Mitchell and Mabuto looked at each other, "How did he perform this magic trick, Doctor?" Martinez asked and pulled up a chair and sat down across from him.

Mabuto looked at him, choosing his words carefully, "You will never believe me in a million years."

Martinez leaned forward, "Try me, Remy. I love a good yarn now and again."

"We always thought Bowers woke something up, ten years ago, by touching the shield, remember?" Martinez nodded. "We have been having some technical problems of late, and a mysterious cloaked figure has been causing mischief."

The room burst into laughter.

"Shut up," Martinez yelled, standing quickly, and then sat back down, calmly, "Continue, Remy, you have my full attention.

Bowers appeared in the Throne room, *Medieval Norse, ancient Chinese design,* he thought as he ran his hands over one of the skulls, and up the back of the Throne, resting a fingertip on one of the arrows he touched it with his fingertip and pricked it, pulled back, then sucked on it to stop the bleeding.

The arrows are an early design of the First Nation tribe in Canada. He slowly worked his way around the Throne, finding Mishophar's crypt, looked it over, Egyptian in design, and walked back to the front, *all could be of one culture, and then deviated.*

In a flash, Mishophar was sitting on his Throne. They stared at each other, Mishophar raised his hand; red lightning bolts flashed from his fingertips, cascading around and surrounding Bowers, but they did not affect him. Bowers laughed.

Mishophar stood, roared, and ran at him. Bowers raised his hands, and Mishophar stopped in mid-air and roared again. Bowers shoved his arms back, and Mishophar flew back over the Throne.

Bowers quickly shifted around the Throne and was hit by many bolts of white lightning, and flew back slamming against the wall, against the remains of Adams's charred shadow.

Mishophar came from behind the Throne with the cowl off his head and hands exposed. He stood over three meters tall, with seven fingers on each hand, and two thumbs, with ghostly white skin, nearly human, without a nose, and a third eye in his forehead, all three were open, the top one was deep black, the other two, a fiery red. No mane on top of his head, but two long horns protruding from his forehead, on each side of his third eye, and back over his head, almost similar to Ram's head on the entrance, his mouth was in a diamond shape, vertical unlike most humans horizontal mouths, and ran from where his nose should have been, and down, under its chin.

He roared again with his opened mouth wide in a diamond pattern, with three rows of canines, small at the ends and larger in the center, saliva flying out and dripping down.

Disgusting, horrifying, Bowers thought, as he stood.

Mishophar charged at him. Bowers cut back into the adjacent room, felt the wall, and heard a click, the wall dropped fast, sealing the room as Mishophar slammed into it, stepped back, and tossed white lightning bolts at the wall. A hole five meters high and about five meters wide, where the shadow of Adams was opened, and he stepped through.

Bowers swung his hand back. Blue bolts hit Mishophar, and tossed him back into the Throne room, "Oh fuck." Bowers yelled as he quickly crawled through a small opening in the back wall, in the lower far corner, and then the wall closed behind him.

Macpherson stepped forward from where Bowers disappeared, "Dan!" she yelled.

"Your friend is all right, he is completing his destiny," The man spoke perfect English, a little over two meters tall, from the other side of the fire. He was holding a long wooden walking stick in his left hand and wearing long white Bedouin robes over his body and head. All they could see was his eyes, his dark blue eyes, and a younger person dressed the same, standing next to him holding his right hand.

"Father are these the ones the Prophetess told us about?" the young girl asked.

He leaned down toward her, "Yes, now hurry, and go tell the elders we have friends." He instructed her, and she ran off back in the direction they were standing near the fire, into the darkness.

The team was in shock and awe by this, Macpherson stepped in front of Hitchcock and Calvin, who had taken up positions in front of the others when the man first spoke.

"Captain Rebecca Macpherson, Earth Alliance. . ."

He cut her off with his right hand raised, then removed the garments from his head and face, "Yes, we have known of you and your friend for some time, Captain. We saw you land eight lunar's ago and the battle up there ten cycles ago." He was completely human, about thirty years of age, just a bit taller than Hitchcock, who was the tallest of their group, just a shy over two and a half meters with long black hair pulled back, and a sight red tint to his skin.

Very good looking, Swanson thought.

Navajo decent, Macpherson thought.

"We thought this planet was uninhabited?" Hitchcock commented.

"We have lived down here for many cycles after the last great death, I do hope you enjoyed the Fassest I made for you, can be very good if cooked properly," He pointed at the remaining meat in the fire.

"Yes, it was good, tasted like an animal we have on Earth, called a cow," Macpherson said.

"Cow?" He questioned.

"An animal, beast of burden," Hitchcock added.

He shook his head, "Yes, we have them here too, and where are my manners, you told me your name, I am Caleb, son of Garth."

"Your speech is the same language as ours, English?" Swanson said.

"We are the same. Evolved the same. As your friend, Dan," Caleb looked at Macpherson for confirmation, and she nodded, "told you, you are the people of the lost colony that left across the sea of stars, egot cycles ago."

Three other figures dressed the same as the girl joined them; she was pulling one by one of his arms in front, "See, I told you."

The team shifted toward the newcomers, "Stop, it's okay, they're friends," Caleb said, shifting between them, with his hands stretched out, "Father, it's all right, they are friends, the ones the Prophetess spoke of danga cycle ago."

The man in the front removed his garments around his face and head. He was a man in his late sixties, with gray hair, but no facial hair, like Caleb, but just shy of two meters, red tint to, his skin also, and was looking intensely at Caleb, who was nodding.

The old man smiled, "Friends!" with his arms open, "Come, come," he waved them to follow, the young girl doing the same.

They all followed, Macpherson moved toward Caleb, "So, I take it, you were the one that helped Dan onto the beach?" She asked as they walked away from the fire.

"Yes,"

Remy explained all that had happened—Waterman Crater, Bowers's return, and the cloaked figure—taking people over and causing damage and mayhem. Martinez took it all in, as he leaned back some in the chair, and crossed his arms.

"Bullshit!" Mr. Red yelled.

Martinez looked over at Mr. Red, "Now, now. It may be what the good Doctor remembers but does not interfere with *my* mission."

"This thing killed one guy, brought him back, destroyed Engineering, and took our people, somehow," Mitchell said quickly.

Mr. Red backhanded him, "May I talk to you, privately?"

Martinez slapped his knees, "Yes, I am parched, you parched, give them some water," he said to Ms. Green and walked out, Mr. Red and Ms. Green followed.

Remy looked closer at the tall Samoan man, "I know you. . . George. . . Tom George."

The Samoan man body-slammed the two guards into the door behind him, body kicked the two behind the Doctor, using Mitchell for support. One of the two guards ran back up, a small man that George slammed into the door, and hit George square in the jaw, but it had no effect. George just stood there. The guard raised his fist again, but George grabbed it, winked, twisted his wrist, and then head-butted him.

Then knelt, and cut the zip ties, both were very confused, "Sorry, Remy, I had to wait to make my move, hope you both were okay."

Remy stood up as George moved over to Mitchell and cut his ties, "What, what?" Mitchell said.

"Orders of Admiral Wainwright—infiltrate, and help Bowers any way I can, he is not here, and you are, so I am."

"This way," Mitchell pushed down on the window ledge. The window and part of the wall section lowered and retracted into the floor; they ran.

Martinez returned with more men and watched as they ran out, and started shooting, turned back toward Ms. Green as Mr. Red joined them, "I had a bad feeling about that one. Find them!" The guards took off.

The three ran down the long leg connected to the hub, and around, Mitchell slapped the doorframe. The door slid open. They ran in as the door closed behind them, just as the guards turned the corner and continued past them, not seeing where they had entered.

Remy was out of breath and collapsed onto the floor.

Mitchell slammed into a few crates, "What's going on, Doc?"

George helped Remy up, "May I present my grandnephew, whom I have not seen in many years, and now a member of Admiral Wainwright's black ops force."

George pulled a canteen out of one of the lockers gave it to Remy nodded toward Mitchell then handed him the canteen.

"Was that the truth you told him, about Bowers and all?"

"Yes," catching his breath, Remy has not run in years, maybe even before Bowers was born, "Where are we, Thomas? I have lost my bearings."

Mitchell slowly leaned his head out and across the large window, trying not to be seen if the guards were near, the "Pumping station."

"Good, we are near the medical bay, I think we can hide better there," Remy said.

"Yes, and I can make contact with the Admiral," George explained.

"We have no Uplink, and I bet they're jamming us," Mitchell said.

"True, but I have a frequency."

Mitchell tapped a few times, and the inner door opened a few centimeters, just enough to see down the corridor in both directions, "Clear," as he waved back toward them, and started to push the door open.

"I'll go first, watch after the old man," George said as he stepped in front of him, slid the door back with ease, and looked out both directions, and waved them to follow.

They inched their way down the corridor, and heard voices off in the distance, George saw a guard around the corner at the medical bay door. He ran, spun around, and tackled him, pushed him back into the room as the door slid open, Remy and Mitchell followed watching the corridor as the door closed.

George slugged the man, and Remy jabbed him with a sedative, "Should be out for hours, more than your punch." They hear noises behind one of the beds. George took off, grabbing Swanson, and she screamed.

"Wait, she's one of us!" Mitchell yelled as he stepped between them.

George stepped back, Mitchell thought he might have growled, "They told us we were the only two here?"

"I hid in cold storage till they cleared this room," she said shaking.

Mitchell picked up a blanket from the bed and put it around her.

Remy reminded George, "Your contact?"

George pulled a small cylinder out of his right pocket, "Ox to Phoenix, over. Ox to Phoenix, over, " Mitchell rolled his eyes, thinking it fit him well, "Ox to Phoenix, over."

"Lone wolf to Ox, report, over."

"Where is Phoenix? Over."

"En route, report, over."

All but Swanson gave a puzzling look, and Mitchell was getting a kick out of all this covert stuff, "Package not at home plate, but near— team away, all but three. Sawbones safe, over," George reported, Remy liked his handle. Mitchell looked at him with an expression of, what are we chopped liver, "Confirm, over."

"Confirmed. Hiroshima twenty, over."

"Hiroshima, twenty, over," George answered. The small device beeped, and George put it back in his pocket.

"Wait one damn minute!" Mitchell said, "Hiroshima? Twenty?"

"In twenty minutes, the other station is going up in smoke, we need to be clear," George advised.

"Other station!" Mitchell questioned.

"No time, we need to move, now. Is there a jeep nearby?" George ordered.

"Yeah, in the other bay, on the other side," Mitchell said pointing with his thumb, at the wall with the beds.

George looked down at Remy, who towered over both, and then back up at Mitchell for answers.

"The catwalk," Swanson suggested.

"Yeah, could work, might be a bit small for you," Mitchell informed him, as he looked over his large frame.

"Show me!"

Mitchell smiled, "We need to get back to the prep room, first."

George shook his head and pointed at the door, "Go!"

Mitchell strolled over, followed by the others, Swanson moved slowly behind them.

Mitchell tapped the panel next to the door, it popped open, and he moved back, and George moved up, looked out, then slid it open, looked round again, and slowly headed out waving back at them.

They quickly made their way back to the prep room. Mitchell tapped the door panel; it closed, and George tapped three more times.

A large metal thud rang out. Mitchell looked at him, "Maglock. . . where?" George demanded.

Mitchell moved a few crates that he had slammed into earlier and pushed on part of the wall, next to the window. It popped out. A long section swung open with a ladder behind it. He pointed up and looked at George with a shit-eaten grin on his face.

"Go!" George ordered.

Mitchell started up the ladder quickly, followed by Swanson, with George's help, then Remy, and finally George, who kicked the wall panel back into place and dropped the small ceiling pane back into place.

"Any luck?" Martinez asked Ms. Green as she entered Command, with Mr. Smith there, he was working under the console at the far end.

"No, but they cannot get far," she reported.

"Get the sensors online and find them!" Martinez ordered.

"Internal sensors are online now," Mr. Smith said as he closed the console and sat, he tapped a few times, "I only count thirty-nine life signs."

"We came with forty! Should be forty-two."

"I can run a diagnostic?" Mr. Smith questions.

"No! Search it again," Martinez ordered, waving at Ms. Green, and stormed out. Mr. Smith looked back over his shoulder, to see if she was still there. She was watching him too. She did not like this. He was too quick with answers. Knowing something was not right she stormed out too.

Mr. Smith turned around and looked out the large window, reached into his lower pocket and pulled the long cylinder out, raised the lid, lifted the switch cover, and switched it on, "Twenty minutes, and he will have no way off this planet."

The timing device Mr. Smith placed earlier switched from 00:00:00 to 00:20:00 and started counting down.

Mitchell kicked the panel out of the ceiling and dropped onto the floor with the metal panel ringing out loud as it crashed on the deck, he looked around, seeing it was clear, stretched back up, and helped Swanson down.

They both helped the Doctor down, but it was not easy. George swung down like a great big ape, Mitchell thought. The jeep sat in the center of the bay like the one Martinez was using, still across from *the Muir.*

Mitchell helped the Doctor in the back; he and Swanson climbed in the front. George quickly tosses through a few crates near the jeep, looking for something, and with surprise, he finds an old M1 Garand with four clips, "Whose is this?" He asked as he took a position in the back, standing up, holding the roll bar.

"Chief Adams liked to shoot it from time to time, let's go!" Mitchell answered.

"Move out!" George yelled and slapped the roll bar.

Mitchell slapped the dashboard. The large outer bay door fell fast and slammed on the ground. He gunned it, and they raced off across the desert as the guards entered, shooting.

The rest, except for Mr. Smith, ran in, "I told you they were still here," Martinez yelled.

Bowers cracked and light, a glow stick trying to see where he was, a dark tunnel, so cramped that he could barely move, he slid slowly, inching his way alone, and dropped down a steep incline, tumbling over, many times, landing hard on a steel deck, looked around, realizing it was a control room, ancient but still a control room.

Rolling over with pain and seeing where he came from, only to see the dome ceiling above him, "Fuck, that hurt," he said under his breath as the stretched and got up. Limping some and finding a small-sized Throne. It was shaped the same as the one in the central chamber. A single glass tabletop in front, about twenty meters squared, for two or three pilots, with squares and circle shapes of different colors, embedded, and he seemed to recognize it. Then in a flash: a blonde man, he kind of knew, and another man with a red tint to his skin were standing next to him at the table, they all were wearing the armor of a Spartan of old Greece, back on Earth, and flying the ship, but he could no tell where he had seen it before, and somewhat understood it. He could see nothing else in the room but a large, oversized window across from the table.

He placed his hand across it, it was not glass; it was a form of plasma, the same plasma shields his fleet used, and he could feel the small charge and plastic touch. He was amazed at the power it took. Looking out, he could see it was hovering over the Pyramid about a hundred meters. But how. he was in the Pyramid, then in the tight tunnel, must have been transported, thinking he may have done it himself. He turned around, finding Mishophar sitting on the Throne, but not with his ghostly white skin, it was just a skeleton.

The city under the Pyramid was huge, running over eight hundred kilometers, Macpherson thought, as she looked it over, interlocking mechanical highways carrying people from place to place, looked as if it had been carved out of the rock, she could see four waterfalls off in the distance, at each of the compass points. Over thirty buildings looked like seven-story apartment structures, like on Earth and Mars, but cut out of the cliff face like the cliff structures in the design of the southwest Pueblo structures. It was amazing, "How long did this take?" she asked turning back toward Caleb.

"It's been here as long as I can remember."

"You stated cycles. Do you mean revolution around your Sun?"

Caleb looked at her with a funny expression; she put her left fist up, "We are here, the Sun here," putting her right fist some distance apart, moving her left fist around her right. "A cycle?"

Caleb nodded and understood, "Yes, K'Tal," he touched her left hand, "Belarus, [B'lar'rus]" he said as he touched her right, and then placed his right fist near her left, "Cha'tain."

She understood. The track stopped quickly, almost tripping her. He caught her, and now she could see this world fully, and it was spectacular.

A real garden, with plants, all kinds of trees, fruits, and vegetables, field after field, it went on for many kilometers, and she had never seen anything like it before, except in vids. She remembered them from Earth before, but not having had them for at least two millennia.

"Welcome to Eden," Caleb said.

"This garden. . ."

"Our world," Caleb informed her with his arms stretched out.

"Is that sunlight?" She asked pointing at the bright area near the cave ceiling.

"No, see the area where it is the brightest, it is a crystal. We believe lava rests on top and illuminates the crystal."

"Always?"

"No, at Kona, it's this bright as now, and Sona, very dim, you will see, later."

"The lava flow decreases. . ."

"Bekka, do you see all this, it's heaven," Swanson said, as she ran up to her with the others. They were all eating different fruits.

Captain Macpherson could not believe her eyes, never in her lifetime had she seen pictures of fields like this, like her great-grandfather's farm way back when, in vids. Taken aback in all its glory, she could breathe. She felt the cool moist clean air for the first time in her life, not that stylized recycled stuff they called air on every ship, station, and those goddamn awful domes on Mars, where she grew up.

Each one called out to her, "You have to see this, Captain."

"Yes, yes, we'll see it all, in time, but first, you were saying about Dan and his destiny?" She demanded and turned back toward Caleb again. A loud bell rang out and resonated in all directions.

"Yes, time for our noon meal, care to join us? I can explain all, there." She nodded and started to follow him, the young girl from earlier, out of her desert wear and in a long black skirt, and white blouse, having longer hair than her Father. Her clothing was that of Earth's fifteen or sixteen century, which Macpherson had read and seen in history books, no buttons down the front, a pullover with long sleeves, and wearing a black vest, it was what she was leading that caused Macpherson to stop and hesitate. At first, she thought they were horses, which have been extinct on Earth for over five hundred years. They had eight legs, four grouped in front and four in back, low, and bulky to the ground, one was black with a large white patch on its face as the long heads of horses had, and the other was red with only a small white strip, which she could not believe, "Fassest?"

Caleb laughed, "Oh no, no, we use these, these are Caval, for getting around and on long-distance travel here and up top."

Embarrassed and glad the young girl spoke first, "Father, Gon, thought she may like to see more before the noon meal."

"Thank you, Mij'ha [Mi'ha], please show the others to the great hall, we will join you shortly," Caleb said as he handed his walking staff to her. Caleb helped Macpherson up into the large saddle, which seated two on the beast. The beast rocked back; Caleb was already on the red one. "Here, take the reins here, and caress her, here," he took her left hand and showing her the reins, patted her right hand on the beast's neck and slapped it hard, the beast settled.

"We don't have animals on Earth like horses anymore."

"Sad, and which twins do you reside on?" He asked leading his beast out, as hers followed.

"We no longer have our twins," Macpherson said.

He looked back at her, "I am sorry, the twin is very beautiful at Soma on the surface when there was life up there."

"Dan told us, after he found the inscriptions on the walls inside the Pyramid, after Misofer, Mesofan."

"Mishophar," he answered patiently correcting her.

"Yes, sometime after his return, a comet crashed into the fifth planet, which became an asteroid field, and one of the twins shifted near the fifth's location."

"Is your world still beautiful as mine was once up top?" Caleb asked.

Macpherson paused and hesitated, "No, we have overused its recourses to a point where it will take longer to repair, but never will, even if we stop doing the damage, now. That is why we came, we found it on our probes, in hopes of starting over, but then we found it a desert world," Macpherson explained.

They came over a ridge, and she saw off in the distance a massive herd of what her mind could only place as Bison from old Earth, on the North American plains, a time called the Ancient West. Caleb whistled with two fingers placed in his mouth. A small branch of the herd turned and hurried toward them. She could see them better now. Unlike the black furry ones of old Earth, these were snow white and over two meters high and about three meters long. Each with stiffer fur, but also looked coarser, with oversized horns nearly a meter wide.

"Fassest, I took part of one of my own from my private stock, and placed it on the spit, for you, we should be getting back now," Caleb said turning his beast around.

Macphersonturned her beast around slowly the way they came, "Your daughter, she's what, about twelve cycles?"

Caleb laughed again, "Oh no, she is only six cycles, we mature faster and age slower since we have been underground."

"I thought you were about thirty?" she said even now more embarrassed.

Caleb smiled, not to offend her, "I celebrated my light, the same day as Bowers appeared on K'Tal recently, after the last time he was here, I am only twenty-five cycles."

"Ch tel?"

"Ka, Ka," he explained and waved his closed fist, fingers near his mouth, to mean a strong syllable, "Taal, Taal," and stretched his fingers out on the last one, "K'Tal." She giggled through her embarrassmient as they headed back.

Bowers stood watching, Mishophar sitting there, not moving. His hands were crossed and intertwined, resting against his chest. Not moving, just there, he walked back slowly back toward the Throne. There was still no movement, not even his eyes glowing, it was just a skeleton. Bowers shifted around the control table and was tossed back against the large window, slammed hard into it, and slipped down to the deck, hard.

Mishophar glided into view from behind the Throne, Bowers stared at him, "How did you get here?" Mishophar demanded.

Bowers rosed up slowly, hovering, and was forced back against the window, he looked back and down at the height, gasping, Mishophar glided up to him, cowl still off his head, raising his right hand to Bowers's face, sparks crackled near his fingertips, "How!"

Bowers was now straining from the weight pressed against his chest, "I . . . don't. . . know!"

Mishophar dropped his hand and walked back toward the Throne. Bowers slammed into the floor, and Mishophar swiped his hand in front of the Throne, his old bones flew up and landed across the room. Mishophar climbed up, spun around again, and sat with elegance.

"This is getting old," Bowers told himself, getting up slowly, using the table for help, and unzipping his jumpsuit a bit, to help him breathe better, "I thought you transported me here."

Mishophar laughed, a hellish laugh as Bowers moved slowly around the table, slowly with each step, stopping on the side facing Mishophar and griping the table tight with his right hand, and twisted his left leg around the other column, tight, and then his right around another. He quickly turned, and slammed his left hand on the tabletop, on a large orange triangle embedded within the table, it lit up, and he grabbed the table tighter with both hands.

The plasma disengaged, the air was forced out and Mishophar's bones flew out, Bowers clinched the table harder, hoping not to fly out himself, seeing the cloaked bones, flying past his head, and hearing Mishophar scream, he touched the triangle again and the screen reappeared.

He looked up, and Mishophar was gone, and he wondered how he knew that would work, as he looked over the table more and started breathing again.

How did I do that? he asked.

The jeep raced across the plateau, George still hanging on the back, as it slammed, and jostled over many rocks and boulders, going airborne and back down, Mitchell regained control and drove on a bit more, Swanson let out a hellish shrieking scream of pain and vanished.

Mitchell slammed on the brakes, and the jeep came to a stop, he and George jumped from the vehicle, George shifted position near where Swanson was with the rife aimed, and Remy's eyes narrowed.

"What the fuck!" Mitchell yelled and looked back at the jeep. George had his rifle pointed at the seat, scoping it out, "I do not think she was who we believe she was, gentlemen," Remy commented, "We had better get to the Pyramid and fast."

Both men quickly climbed back into the jeep and sped off.

Martinez slammed the center console in Command, "Damn it all. . ." Out the window he saw the ridge across the plateau explode, shaking the room and station, he was slammed back into the door.

"Quake!" Ms. Green yelled as she slammed into him.

"No, that was a bomb!" He quickly tapped the console. The center window melted and showed a fireball erupting over Schmitt's Gorge and moved in slowly to show the outer bay and the two shuttles destroyed, fires everywhere, and with a few bodies lying on the ground. The bomb had completely decimated the station and over half the cliff face atop it.

Martinez's eyes widen, "No!"

Ms. Green watched as her Father slammed his fist on the console again, he had never given this much concern for something that was not family. Mr. Smith came running in and stopped fast, seeing the look on Martinez's face, and seeing the hate in Martinez's eyes, "You, you did this!" Mr. Smith ran back the way he came, "Get him!"

Ms. Green pulled her pistol from her waistband and took off after him. Mr. Smith hurried down the long corridor, hitting the walls a few times and trying not to trip, and entered the cargo bay. Mr. Red turned toward him after talking with two guards as he ran in. Mr. Smith landed a left-handed punch on his chin, pushing him back into the two guards, then jumped into a jeep, and sped off, Ms. Green following behind, firing.

Mr. Red joined her outside, nursing his jaw, "What was that?"

She slugged her Brother hard with her pistol, "Idiot, we had another spy, don't you check your people out better!"

"Sergei hired the first squad." Mr. Red answered whipping blood off his chin.

She taps the base of her ear, "He's gone."

The jeep sped off, Mr. Smith not knowing where he was going. She had hit him, bleeding from his right shoulder, with lots of blood, the jeep zigzags across the plateau and crashed into a large boulder, flipped its front end up and over the large bolder, and landed hard on the plateau. Mr. Smith dragged himself out as far as he could with his good arm, rolled over onto his back, pulled out the small COM device inside his jacket, "Lone wolf to Phoenix, over. Hiroshima complete, I am out and down, repeat, I am down, over," as he fell back onto the desert floor.

"Confirmed, I am planet side now, over," Admiral Wainwright replied.

The dining hall was huge, went for over a kilometer, and like everything else there, carved out of stone, Macpherson noticed as they entered through the two large wooden doors, which spanned over five meters high. Her team was sitting on pillows and rugs on the floor, food of all kinds in bowls and large goblets filled with wine and water on top, a long marble table barely off the ground. Others of Caleb's people sat around the larger table, and at other tables nearby dressed like Mij'ha or Gon at smaller ones around the room, three Fassest were turning on three huge spits at the far end of the room, she also heard harp and flute music playing. Swanson stood and waved at her from the far end of the table to join them, where she was sitting with Gon and Mij'ha, who was waving at them with excitement.

Gon was an older man, late into his eighties, she thought, his left eye, most of his left forehead, and head covered with a metal plate. A small amount of gray hair on his head remained and was wearing a large furry section of a Fassest on his right shoulder, all she could see from his seated position, he was smiling and missing most of his teeth with both hands up extended in friendship, "Welcome, welcome," he said spilling a large drink from his goblet, and spilling most and laughing, "Sit, drink, eat, you are welcome."

Swanson met her halfway and guided them back as two female Edenits, placed white plates with Fassest stakes and many assorted vegetables down in front of her and Caleb, she could recognize most of them from Earth: potatoes, carrots, and some squashes, but not the blue and silver ones.

Caleb smiled and encouraged her to eat, as he picked up a two-pronged metal fork, and ate some of the vegetables.

"You spoke of Dan's destiny?" Macpherson asked again, looking first at Caleb and then toward Gon.

Gon slapped the table, still laughing, "Once Mij'ha told me, your friend was able to read the markings in the Pyramid, and we have all been taught the words of the Prophetess, over the danga cycle, of a warrior, who comes home from beyond the sea of stars. Once the Ancient one arose, and the warrior would defeat him because of his link to us."

"Link to us. . . you?" Walker-Swanson asked.

"You are all family; the lost tribe many egot cycles ago, you still carry markers with us, when Mishophar attacked him. Your friend, Bowers, gained the power to stand up to him," Gon explained.

The team looked at each other in confusion, not understanding many of the words he was using. Hitchcock broke their silence and confusion first, "Yes, oh yes, of course, the same DNA markers," he explained, and Macpherson nodded.

"And when Bowers was hit the first time, his dormant DNA markers restarted to give him an even advantage," Gon continued.

"Couldn't Dan also die?" Macpherson asked Gon, with trepidation in her voice.

Gon giggled louder and with more spirit from his drunkenness, looked straight at her, "Maybe sooo."

She shot a look of horror at Caleb. Two men take the Swansons and walk them over to a large open area behind the spits and start dancing, each raising their legs high with the rhythm of the music, they both look back at Macpherson, as if what they should do.

"Caleb, I. . . we can't lose him."

CHAPTER TEN

PREVENTING A COUP

JESSICA WAINWRIGHT WAS CRYING bittersweet from the news of Bowers being alive, the door chimed, and wiped her eyes, "Yes."

Donovan entered, "Jessie, you all right?" and sat down next to her, "You know he is all right; Bowers has a knack for getting out of things. You remember that time when he got out of your Father's house that night without your Dad finding out on New. . ." and burst out laughing.

She jumped up, and crossed the room behind her desk, "We have a mission to complete, no time for reminiscing," she yelled.

"Captain, we were arriving in the *Triton system*," *Gamma* advised.

Jessica Wainwright wiped the last of her tears away and looked down at the pictures, "On our way," straightened her jumpsuit and looked back over at Donovan, and they left.

Arriving on the bridge, "Ma'am, we have registered a sizable explosion in the northern hemisphere, a few hundred kilometers from the *Gamma II* research station," Watson advised from the left chair, near the elevator, with a massive cloud still above the surface on the screen.

"Any contact from the *Gamma II* station?" Jessica Wainwright asked.

"Negative, our communications are still being jammed," Galloway said from the right console near the elevator.

Jessica Wainwright already knew that was the job of *the Roosevelt,* "So, we can't tell who is on the planet and where?"

Galloway turned and looked at the Captain, "No, Ma'am."

"The equipment is ready, you asked for?" Watson commented.

Galloway nodded and followed Donovan and the Captain out, "Mr. Watson, you have the CON." Jessica Wainwright ordered as Watson shifted from the chair on the left of the elevator to the center one.

Entering the shuttle bay, Watson called out over the COM, "*The Roosevelt* has entered the system, Captain."

"Place us in orbit behind *Trinity's* moon and wait," Jessica Wainwright ordered as she climbed into one of the two oversized cargo shuttles. Red lights flashed, as the two shuttles lifted slowly off the deck, one after the other, passing through the transparent field holding back the vacuum of space, "Omega alert, Commander."

"Understood, Ma'am," Watson replied over the COM as alarms rang out, crews hustled around the deck cleaning up and returning to the ship as the bay doors closed.

"Omega alert! All personal to Omega alert!" *Gamma* called out.

The summit was taking place at the main Founders Dome on Mars, on the *Tharsis Plateau,* a concrete dome in the capital inside the *Tharsis Plateau* crystal dome. All representatives from Earth, Mars, *IO,* and colonies outside the system were meeting. This was a conference to debate and discuss the future of all off-world colonies and the distribution of resources. The President's shuttle slowly glided down onto the large pad outside the Dome, which already had representatives from all over the systems. The elongated white-with-blue-trim shuttle that seats twelve, with only the symbol of the Earth President on the shuttle's hatch, gently came to a rest on the pad. Senator Macomb, Admiral Fitzsimmons, and a Military entourage stood off from the shuttle's pad with other dignitaries. Senators, Military personnel, and Colonists waited. The shuttle's hatch slowly rose, and Military personnel came to attention. The Marine Corps band starts playing the old nineteenth-century song "Dixie" instead of "Hail to the Chief," with a large tabernacle choir behind the band singing out loud:

Oh, I wish I was in the land of cotton,
Old times there are not forgotten.
Look away, look away, look away Dixie Land!
In Dixie's Land, where I was born in,
Early on one frosty morning.
Look away, look away, look away Dixie Land!

I wish I was in Dixie. Hooray! Hooray!
In Dixie's Land I'll take my stand,
To live and die in Dixie.
Away, away, away down south in Dixie!
Away, away, away down south in Dixie!

Senator Macomb stood with a big smile on his face, with his arms stretched out, in a white gentlemen's suit, holding a walking cane, singing, and enjoying the old song, he looked over at Fitzsimmons, still in his dressed blues, and hating it, and does not wish to be there, but he had a job to do.

The President and Senator Cooper stepped out of the shuttle, waving, and the President whispered to Cooper, "I thought we agreed on my theme song?"

"We did, but you know Macomb, he has his hands in everything on Mars," Cooper answered as they continued waving to the crowd, and hearing all the cheers and support, but only if they knew what was coming next.

Macomb waved them on into the grand hall, with Fitzsimmons carrying an oversized metal briefcase.

In a room off the main chamber, while all the others wait for the President's speech, he and Senators Macomb and Cooper, and Admiral Fitzsimmons, with four guards, enter. Cooper and the President sat on a couch, with blue drapes covering the walls, across the room, a green Velour four-person couch, both feeling something was not right.

Senator Macomb picked up two champagne glasses and handed one to the President, "Mr. President, Admiral Fitzsimmons has a document for you to look over before your speech."

Fitzsimmons rested the briefcase on the same table Macomb had picked up the glasses from and handed him a blue tri-fold document, and the four guards raised their rifles.

The President stood up fast, "What is the meaning of this!"

"By executive order one one three eight, Earth year twenty-two oh five, for conspiracy to overthrow the Earth Alliance and gaining Military resources, and troops for your use, you are under arrest, Sir," Fitzsimmons ordered.

Cooper stood joining him quickly, and then touched a button on his watch. He and the President fade away slowly in a green mist. Fitzsimmons looked back at Macomb.

A large shuttle landed near the blast site in Schmitt's Gorge. Soldiers exited and headed off into what was left of the station, all wearing tan, and brown Camos, desert wear, Admiral Wainwright exited, wearing Camos also with a pistol holster on his waistband, "Secure what's left of the station!"

With a beep from his pocket, he removed a small COM device, "Lone wolf to Phoenix, over, Hiroshima complete, I am out and down, repeat, I am down, over," Mr. Smith called out.

"Confirmed, I am planet side, now, over," Admiral Wainwright replied, putting it back in his pocket. He waved at two technicians setting up a drone, which looked like a small glider plane.

"Get that thing airborne, and find my Son, now!" He ordered as the small gray drone hovered slowly up, gaining altitude, and flew off over the cliff wall.

Davidson ran up, "Sir, no survivors, station is empty."

Admiral Wainwright waited, as the technicians watched the screen on a makeshift metal table, watching the drone continue over the cliff wall and out over the plateau, just the barren plateau, then one of the technicians pointed at the screen, "Sir, you should see this?"

On the screen, the Pyramid, and above, hovering was the massive Ancient ship.

Admiral Wainwright looked at the screen, "My God. Plot that point and find my Son, Damn it!"

The drone slowly turned and headed off to the north, over the Pyramid, and continued across the plateau, moving slowly, and came upon a crash site.

The screen zoomed in and showed Mr. Smith, hanging partly out of a jeep, "Yes, there he is, plot that! Davidson, where out of here, get the vehicles!"

Three jeeps converge on the crash site. A female medical technician jumped out with the Admiral and hurried up to the unconscious Mr. Smith. The Admiral hurried and pulled his Son out of the jeep, holding him, and then laid him down on the ground, with his head on his thigh, "Matt, I am here, wake up."

The female medical technician took out her screen from a pack and ran it over him, and then pulled out a small rod, and slowly ran it over his right arm, the blood slowed and stopped, and then waved at two others holding a stretcher.

Davidson hurried and handed the Admiral a screen from the drone. He stepped away from his Son and the medical technician, and two others placed Matt Wainwright on the stretcher and then placed him on the front hood of one of the jeeps. On the screen, he saw another jeep racing across the desert toward them fast. Davidson pointed off to the Admiral's right, the direction they were coming from; he zoomed in on the screen and saw Remy and George, "Okay, we make camp here!"

George saw the makeshift camp, "Stop!" and scanned for the Admiral, who was standing around a few others in one of the makeshift open tents. The Admiral looked up hearing the commotion of the jeep skidded to a stop and they hurried out toward them.

Mitchell helped the Doctor out of the jeep, as the Admiral ran up, "Report, Major."

Major George faced the Admiral from across the Jeep, standing at attention, "We just escaped from Martinez's group, Bowers is at the Pyramid with the rest of Macpherson's crew, and I got these two out after Martinez's team assaulted the station.

Not bringing up what happened with Swanson, if it was Swanson, choosing not to concern that aspect with the Admiral.

The Admiral turns to the Doctor, "How is Dan, Remy?"

"Not a day older and finishing what he started, like he always did," Remy answers.

The Admiral nodded and waved his arm high toward an area where Davidson was waiting, who was a few meters away and standing next to three oversized rockets, waiting to be launched, each with a white, red, and blue stripe along the side of each white rockets, and they launched them. They flew high into the atmosphere. Exploding and lighting up the sky that was already bright, first red, then white, and finally blue.

The two oversized shuttles from *the Roanoke* hovered gently down to the plateau and landed a few meters off from the base camp. The shuttle's hatch rose. Captain Jessica Wainwright exited, hugged her father, and then came to attention.

The Admiral's plan was coming together now, to help Bowers complete his original mission, and stop Martinez.

"Two exceptionally large shuttles just landed on the plateau near the Pyramid," Ms. Green advised Martinez, both still in Command.

How?" Martinez said still looking out the window, then looked over the screen, and nodded his head, "I knew Wainwright could not sit on the sidelines after learning what I had done. Have Mr. Red assemble the men, we are moving out in ten minutes."

"Moving out, where?" she asked.

"The Pyramid, Commander Bowers has chosen the battlefield." He answered as Ms. Green left. Martinez looked back out the window, "He will be no help to you, Dan. I have you now, checkmate." Still believing he still had the upper hand.

The outer chamber was in an uproar; the President was over a half hour late in giving his speech. Fitzsimmons, now with a screen and running it over the area where the President and Cooper were standing, took the cigar from his mouth, "Nothing, just nothing."

"Dead?" Macomb asked.

The Vice President entered, African American in her late fifties, some gray in her hair, "Gentlemen, where is the President? He is over a half hour late for his speech," Vice President Sonja Appleton asked, wearing a gray pantsuit.

"Madam Vice President, I must report, we were about to arrest the President and Senator Cooper for conspiracy and coup to take over the government, the President, Senator Cooper, and Admiral Martinez were starting, but they just vanished," Fitzsimmons answered, handing her the warrant from his back pocket, and stood at attention.

Taking the warrant, she skimmed through it, "These are heavy charges, Admiral. I do hope you have the evidence to back it up," Vice President Appleton commented, as Macomb laid three large blue oversized folders on the table, from the briefcase, "you said, they just disappeared, how?"

"Yes, Senator Cooper pressed a button on his watch as I was handing the warrant to the President, and they vanished in a green mist." Fitzsimmons answered.

"They must have one of the alien technologies, found in the *Andromeda Galaxy*. Thought we had it locked up tight," Vice President Appleton stated.

The Admiral and Macomb looked at each other, very confused. They were aware of the weapons, but not where they were stored, "Your orders, Ma'am?" Fitzsimmons asked.

"Find them!"

"Go check on your brother, Princess, he's over there," showing her the makeshift medical tent, Remy was coming out of and with some blood on his white jacket. She ran, and he turned back toward Mitchell and Major George, "So, let me get this straight, Son. Bowers woke up an Ancient thing, and it has been wreaking havoc?"

"How. . . ?" Mitchell started.

"I am a three-star Admiral, boy. There is nothing I don't know."

"Yes, Sir, my team is at the Pyramid, and I wish to join them to help." Mitchell burst out.

"You will, Son. We will all have Bowers's back. How many does Martinez have, Major?"

"Maybe twenty, now, after your Son, the Colonel had killed the others in the blast."

"Davidson!" Admiral Wainwright yelled. The kid ran up, "Has Remy checked my Son out? Can he move out with us?"

"Ask him yourself, Sir," Davidson answered, thinking the kid was out of line, and then turned where Davidson was pointing, and saw Matt, Jessica, and Remy walking over, hugging each other like a family reunion.

"So, Remy, how's my boy?"

He pressed his lips together, and looked at Matt Wainwright, "It was touch and go there for a minute, but I got the bullet out, and he is fit as a fiddle."

"Okay, Colonel, you and George muster the troops!" Admiral Wainwright ordered Matt Wainwright and the Major, and they headed off.

"So, what's your plan, Admiral?" Mitchell asked.

"We will gain access into the Pyramid and find Commander Bowers, Captain Macpherson, and her team, and help in any way we can, in stopping Martinez and his plan for *this* planet. I hope you brought more men; I only have about twenty."

"Double that, more in orbit, and equipment to repair the *Gamma II* station," Macpherson answered.

"Thank you, his people and that thing has trashed it, we have not been able to Uplink with Earth for two weeks," Mitchell informed them.

"Why do you think we are here, Son? *The Roosevelt* has been jamming this sector for two months."

"And now in orbit," she added.

"So, we have less time than I thought, *the Roanoke* near for a hot exaction, if called for?"

"Standing by, behind *Trinity's* moon, two beeps, and it will be in orbit."

Davidson stepped up with the screen for the drone. "Sir, he is on the move."

The Admiral looked at the screen, two large vehicles raced across the desert, "Colonel! Are we ready to move out!"

Both shuttle's rear doors opened, and two jeeps and two oversized vehicles emerged, "And a few toys I thought you would need," with Galloway and Donovan, and a few others from *the Roanoke* in the larger vehicles.

He smiled at his Daughter, looked over at his Son in the jeep now in Cammos, and George in the other, "Pack it up, Davidson, we're moving out!"

Martinez's group was now heading for the Pyramid, knowing Admiral Wainwright was near, but it did not concern him. He knew the trap was set, but Martinez did not know he was about to fall into a trap, a trap made for him.

Bowers was watching all of this from inside the ship, through a holographic screen above the table, watching both teams racing toward the Pyramid, hoping Bekka and her team were safe, and knowing very soon that all hell was going to break loose on *Gamma II*.

Before Caleb could answer her, the hall shook violently. A young man whispered into Gon's ear, but he waved him off, "Just tell us what's happening!"

"Two forces have started a conflict on the surface, near the old Pyramid."

Macpherson did not know who it could be and stood up, followed by Calvin and Hitchcock, "I need to get back up there."

Another blast rocked the hall. The quake rolled through Eden, and people scrambled everywhere, rock, dust, and debris falling all around.

"Get to the shelters!" Gon yelled.

"This way!" Caleb yelled, taking Macpherson by her hand, and running out of the great hall. Hitchcock and Calvin followed, Walker-Swanson saw them leaving and waved to her wife and they ran after them.

He led them out, cutting through the crowd of people who were running in all directions. A pillar nearly hit Calvin, but Hitchcock pulled him back. They ran into a small room near the hall, a young man sat wearing a silver jumpsuit in front of a console, unlike the rest of Eden, which was agrarian; this room was more like their own technology, "Transport us to the surface." Caleb ordered.

"Negative, Gon's ordered," the young man answered.

"Now!" leading Macpherson to a platform across the room, with two circular pads, each glowing white, "Keep your hands near your body, and breathe," Macpherson realized it was an elevator, and it rocketed up.

The lights on each level flash and flash faster with each level, but it was going too fast. Macpherson wanted to scream but nothing came out, and she passed out.

The team watched as the platform shot up as another blast hit the complex and the console exploded, tossing the young man across the room.

"Did they make it?" Swanson yelled, as the ceiling came crashing down, rocks and tiles, fell around them, and finally the base of the platform exploded.

The last image Swanson saw is everything going white.

CHAPTER ELEVEN

GAMBIT

"DANNY, STAY NEAR ME OR HASSAN," Carolyn Bowers instructed *her young son. She was in her mid-sixties, with graying hair with a small amount of black, blue jeans and a white T-shirt, and Bedouin cap, and scarf around her neck.*

Carolyn Bowers was on a major Archeological dig of her life at the Sippar dig site in the Iraqi confederation of the Saudi Arabian States, on Earth in 2244 along with her young son, Daniel Bowers. Her team had just unearthed the largest Pyramid ever found. It stood over two hundred kilometers high, eleven times higher than the Pyramid at Giza in Egypt and was buried for over eight millennia. It had taken her and her team about three years to blow away the sand and dig out the rest; there was no writing or pictographs on the outside. She could see from the entrance, carved out of the stone after its construction, unlike most Pyramids she had found or explored.

At the top of the entrances stood a six-meter tall Ram's head also carved out of the structure. At thirteen, Daniel Bowers dressed in short tan pants, a white dress shirt, and suspenders, was in awe with this find, and like many times on a dig with his Mother, he was like a kid in a candy store.

Hassan Robdda was the lead Archeologist for the Confederation of States, her mentor, teacher, and friend. She had known him since her first dig in her early years when she was in graduate school. He was not a tall man, stood just shy of five feet tall, a large man with a scraggly beard. Dressed in black pants and a white dress shirt, suspenders with Bedouin robes and cap, and was at most times one of

Daniel's babysitters. Daniel got into more mischief than most kids did before the age of thirteen, and she could never really discipline him. He was her baby, other than shipping him off to another family member for some time. However, he found himself wanting to know more about this world of the past than at any time in his lifetime.

Something pulled at him when he saw the Ram's head, it pulled deep at him inside. Young Daniel moved closer to the Pyramid, slowly walking down the steps with his Mother and Robdda, and a few workers. He needed to get inside; it felt like home, which he had never really had growing up, and to this point in his life because his parents always traveled. Either he was with one of them or both when they did travel together, which was rare. Or he would stay with one of his sisters or an Aunt, his Mother's sister, or Remy, which he preferred personally.

"Danny, watch now, there is always a lock and key, and it's not always obvious, but it will be there," Carolyn told the young boy.

He watched as his Mother and Robdda brushed the excess dirt off the wall of the entrance, revealing a map of the Sol System, with all eleven planets. They looked at each other with confusion, primarily because of the twin planets where Earth sat, knowing there were only ten planets in the galaxy, and a fifth planet, where the asteroid belt sat.

She ran her finger over the map and found the fourth one. One of the twins was raised a bit more than the other, and a path to the fifth. She pushed it slowly. It moved over to the fifth, and it locked into place with a loud clicking sound.

"Yes!" Bowers thought and looked down at the Pyramid from the Ancient ship. "They are the same Pyramids, just a difference in sizes."

His Mother opened her Pyramid the same way he did with this one. Bowers had confirmed both Pyramids were identical, except in height, as the one his Mother found in Sippar, as a child, and the slide Professor Ranko showed him thirteen years ago. The feeling of home as a child was not for the one on Earth but for this one; he was home. Earth was the Lost Outpost after he read the walls inside the Pyramid, but something awoke inside him, too. Still, new images appear in his mind. Faster than before, all he could see were brief images, the building of the Pyramid, the fleet that found Earth, and the Meteorite that hit the fifth planet back in his Galaxy. He realized he was becoming K'Talian or something more. Did Mishophar wake up something when he first hit him with his power back on the first day, or ten years ago when he touched the force field?

Like when his memories were first coming back after reading *Gamma's* files, about him and the station, there were other things too, like an earlier life, which he did not remember or had been dormant in humanity for over ten millennia and himself. How he matched Mishophar in his powers in the Throne room? Knowing how he dropped the shield of the large window from the table, or the force field ten years ago, and how more was coming back to him, how the table looked familiar, and this control room.

He ran his hand over a large red square with a small green triangle set inside. The lights came on fully. He could now see the room better and could search it more. At first, he only saw the table and the Throne, but now with the lights fully on, he could see the whole room, there were two other tables, similar to the front one but half the size, along the back wall. There was a nine-foot-tall archway cut out of the wall next to them, an adjunct room. He looked over the tables and then poked his head into the other room. A chirping noise stared from the front table.

He saw a small red circle flashing and touched it, the chirping stopped, and the hologram changed, now showing Wainwright's team heading for the Pyramid. With instinct, he slowly moved his fingertips around the red circle, the image zoomed in, and he could see Jessie.

Another chirping sound and he touched the red circle again. The image changed to a different team heading to the Pyramid, circling again, it zooms in again, and he sees Martinez.

Bowers sat back on the Throne, realized Martinez was there, and wanted it all for himself but seeing Jessie, still as lovely as ever, he thought, but he would also take any help he could get when it came to Martinez. He quickly stood up, touched a large green oval, and a green beam shot out from the underside of the Ancient ship, shooting out and across the plateau, and changed shape from a thin beam into a wall, ten kilometers high and sixty kilometers wide in front of Martinez, and his convoy, blocking their way to the Pyramid.

Martinez raised his hand. Mr. Red slammed on the brakes, halting the convoy, and Martinez stood up looking over the front window of the large vehicle, looking out at the massive green wall in front of them. Then climbed down, putting his hand up. *It's solid and warm.* Martinez thought.

"Screen, Pilar?" Martinez yelled.

Pilar climbed down with a screen and handed it to him. He ran it over the wall, up and down, side to side, and then tapped it a couple of times, "Hmm, very interesting," He said to himself and handed it back to her.

She looked over the screen, "Power source unknown, cannot tell where it's coming from, but it's here," Pilar reported.

"And will be mine, soon," Martinez stated.

Admiral Wainwright put his hand up and stopped the convoy only a few kilometers from the Pyramid, which was now in sight, and they could see the long green wall off in the distance on the far side of the Pyramid. Then he saw it, the massive Ancient ship still hovering over the Pyramid, with a single thin green beam pulsing toward the massive green wall, "Oh my God!" He said as removed his sunglasses.

Jessica Wainwright stood up in the back of the jeep, holding the roll bar, and removed her sunglasses also, "It's got to be Daniel."

Matt and Admiral Wainwright looked back at her as if she had lost her mind. A hologram of Bowers appeared a couple of meters in front of the jeep. She smiled longingly and pointed; they turned and saw him. The Admiral climbed down and looked up at him, "You have some explaining to do, Mister?"

"Yes, Sir, in due time, but first, please move your convoy to the entrance side of the Pyramid, we do not have much time, the power reserves in the ship will not keep the wall up long. The Pyramid has more power to keep the shield up around it, and you all will be safer under it." Bowers explained standing at a height of six meters.

Remy smiled and Admiral Wainwright climbed back into the jeep and waved them all to move out and drive through the hologram of Bowers as he disappeared.

"Being me the case, Rafe!" Martinez ordered.

Rafe jumped out of the large vehicle and ran back to the second truck, climbed in, and slid a large silver case out, the one Martinez dropped back on *IO* for Mr. Jones. Two mercenaries placed it on the ground. One meter tall by two and a half meters wide, and one and a half meters deep, the two mercenaries grabbed it and ran, followed by Rafe. They set it down near Martinez, he unclamped the lid and opened it.

Pilar looked with curiosity as Martinez pulled two, one and a half meters-long black tubing, metal in appearance, and connected them. Rafe brought out a three-meter squared flat piece, also metal in appearance, with a one-and-a-half-meter circular shape jutting up to hold the tubing. Martinez placed the tubing into the housing, and onto the base plate, as Rafe twisted it tight.

Martinez pulled a small black box from the case, "Stand clear!" Martinez yelled as they all moved back behind the second vehicle, taking cover.

"What is that?" Pilar asked.

"I found this toy on *my* excursions to the *Andromeda Galaxy*," He answered here, "and I have found nothing it can't bring down."

He lifted the small lid on top of the black box and opened it, three red buttons inside, in a triangular shape. He pressed the top button.

A loud tone started rising and became so loud that most of the mercenaries and Pilar covered their ears. A bright circular ball blasted up about five meters and exploded, lighting up the sky, brighter. The wall arced and flickered, then disappeared. Martinez smiled.

They reached the entrance side of the Pyramid, and the sky exploded with a bright light, "What the fuck was that?" Admiral Wainwright yelled. Just as the shield flashed red to show it was now around them, and the Pyramid, and closed before another blast hit.

"Sir?" Major George said, pointing behind the Pyramid with a pair of binoculars. Admiral Wainwright climbed out of his jeep and took the binoculars from him, and saw Martinez celebrating and the weapon, "That son of a bitch has one the weapons!"

"Weapons?" Jessica Wainwright asked.

"One of many weapons that his team found on the outer planet of the *Andromeda Galaxy,* on his last mission before retiring, but I locked it up."

"As I have said before, Admiral, he has his own agendas," Bowers said, standing behind them. They turned. Jessica Wainwright grabbed him. They hugged, holding each other close, kissing, trying to make up for lost time.

Admiral Wainwright cleared his throat to get their attention, as a Father of a teenage daughter would, cleaning his gun. Matt and Remy smiled, "Report, Mister?" Admiral Wainwright ordered.

Jessica stepped back and fixed her lipstick. Bowers stepped up, "After I learned, I had woken something up ten years ago, and found out Earth is a Lost Outpost of this world. We have come home. . ."

"That is all well and good, but I am asking about that," Admiral Wainwright cut him off and pointed up at the Ancient ship, then out across the plateau, "and what the hell, is he doing!"

"That is what launched ten years ago, and somehow I can operate it. Martinez is here because like you, he learned I was here and alive, and as I have said before, he wants all this new technology and weapons for his own, mostly for money. He has a plan for the *Andromeda Galaxy,*" Bowers explained.

The shield flashed again, an explosion on the outer side, but the shield held it back, but the ground shook hard, shaking like a powerful quake, all held on to a vehicle or someone else, Jessica Wainwright grabbed Bowers.

"Sir?" Major George pointed back toward Martinez. Admiral Wainwright took the binoculars again and saw Martinez next to an oversized slim-barrel cannon, one and a half meters tall, and the barrel over two meters, firing another red bolt. The red bolt slammed into the shield, shaking the ground, more powerful than the first.

"How long will it hold?" Jessica Wainwright asked.

"This way!" Bowers called out, running back toward the entrance, with all following him, down the steps and into the main chamber, and at the far wall, he slammed his palm on the symbol, the eye of

Re, and part of the wall rose about a meter wide, opening on to a dark room, "Go!"

Jessica Wainwright and the Admiral look back questioning him, "Trust me, now, go!"

She kissed him, and they ran in. He slammed the eye of Re again, a bright light flashed from inside the dark room, and the wall descended, and Bowers vanished.

Martinez pleased with his work watches the shield weakening as the cannon continued firing, "Okay, that's enough. Pack it up, we're moving out."

Three mercenaries take apart the cannon into three pieces, the barrel, the housing, and the base, and pack it back into the first oversized vehicle. Rafe took apart the alien weapon and placed it back into the case. The two mercenaries that brought it now returned it to the second vehicle, and the convoy moved out.

A green light from the Ancient ship hit the ground in front of the convoy, The convoy stopped, and another green light exploded, "That's far enough, Admiral." Bowers commanded.

Martinez and his team heard Bowers's voice but did not see him, "Old friend, where are you?" Martinez said.

"We were never friends, maybe comrades in arms, and this planet will not be yours, nor the technology."

"Let's talk about it, Son."

"I am not your Son."

Martinez vanished. Pilar screamed. Rafe floored the large vehicle and raced to the Pyramid with a fury.

Martinez appeared in front of the large crater, he jumped, turned, and saw he was under the shield, and in front of the Pyramid. Then turned back and looked over and down into the crater, picked up a small rock, and tossed it over, waiting to hear it hit the bottom, but it did not.

"I am on to you this time, Admiral," Bowers said. Martinez turned fast, "I know about you wanting to use this planet as a staging point, but what is going on in *Andromeda?*"

Martinez laughed, "Son, the riches we could have, the riches I have seen in *Andromeda*. That blast weapon is only the first, and that ship," pointing up at the Ancient ship, "is just the first of many, and the profits we could make just on it."

"I am not in this for profit and never will be, and this, like the knowledge of Lord Carnarvon and Howard Carter, who found the tomb of King Tut in the Valley of the Kings, back in the first half of the twentieth century. Or the tombs of the Shelite [She'lite] people discovered by Allen Tiran, and Lady Sally Cooperson from the UK on *Orion Six,* fifty years ago, or any find we make, it's to better mankind, not profit from it."

Martinez laughed again, "You will not stop me." Martinez ran at him and tackled him. They rolled over a couple of times and struggled. Martinez gained the advantage and hit him three times across the jaw. Bowers coughed up blood, and with blood on his face spat back at him. Martinez raised his fists above his head and slammed them down; Bowers got his leg out from under and kicked him aside and tossed him off.

Martinez stood. The shield flickered again and arced. They watched the red shield slowly lower from above, around, and blast into the surface, and the ground exploded, shaking again, both losing their footing.

Martinez saw his team approaching and ran back at Bowers. Bowers twisted, dropped, and kicked him; they wrestled more. Bowers broke the grip. Martinez slugged him repeatedly. Bowers hit him a couple of times along his jaw, and Martinez tossed him off to the side.

Martinez ran at him, Bowers blocked him with his feet and flipped him up, and over into the gorge. Martinez yelled and flew up and over into the gorge, Pilar cried out, and watched her Father go over the edge. Rafe pulled his pistol and started shooting, and they stopped the vehicle, "You son of a bitch!"

Reaching the surface of the two circular pads, Macpherson fell, and passed out, and Caleb saw Bowers, and tackled Rafe, knocking him to the ground. The mercenaries took off after him to assist, and another green bolt fired from the Ancient ship and landed between Caleb and the mercenaries. All look up, and then Rafe broke away from Caleb, he climbed into one of the jeeps and sped off.

"Nobody move!" Jessica Wainwright ordered from the Ancient ship.

Macpherson awoke and saw Pilar climbing down from the large vehicle, reaching for her pistol, but she grabbed it first, "Hold it right there, you heard her, nobody move!"

Bowers stood, smiled, and looked up, "Press the yellow star, Jessie." The Wainwrights, Major George, and the team appeared back on the plateau with rifles drawn.

"Move them over there and hold them," Admiral Wainwright instructed.

Jessica Wainwright and Macpherson moved toward Bowers, "Jessie, this is Rebecca Macpherson, Bekka, an old friend and student of mine from the academy, and she has been a big help here." They both nodded.

"You killed my Father!" Pilar called out from the group, kneeling with zip ties on her wrists, shoving at the soldier holding her.

"Bring her here," Bowers ordered. Major George picked her up and walked her over, as Admiral Wainwright joined them, "I am sorry, but it was his fault," Bowers said. She spat on him. Bowers wiped his face. Admiral Wainwright waved Major George to return her to the rest, "No, wait." Bowers looked over the edge, and Caleb stepped up near, also looking over, "Look for yourself, Pilar. He may have survived; there is an ocean under this plateau."

"And not, in this area there is a section of thick rock between the surface and the ocean," Caleb advised.

All but Macpherson looked at him, wondering who he was and where he came from, "I am sorry, Dan, this is Caleb, the one who made the fire and left us the meat under the Pyramid. There is a grand society and world underground."

Bowers nodded, looked back at Matt Wainwright, then Caleb again, and for a moment both men were dressed as Spartans, and he realized both men were with him on the ship, in the past, when he recognized the ship and her controls, "They're all yours, Admiral."

Pilar took one last look at Matt Wainwright, realizing she was right about him, as Major George walked her past Matt Wainwright toward the rest of the oversized vehicles and placed her inside.

Remy and Mitchell join the group near the crater, "So everyone is all right?" Mitchell asked.

"Yes, except for Chief Adams, Mishophar killed him, when we all met up again inside the Pyramid, Hitchcock informed me," Macpherson answered.

Remy shook his head, "and what is this about an underground society?"

"Yes, huge, and magnificent. . . Caleb, the blasts, your people, my team! How do we get down there?" Macpherson asked.

"Before you all return to your teams, we need to stop *the Roosevelt*, Jessie," Admiral Wainwright said returning and looking at Jessica Wainwright. She took her COM from her pocket. Pressed the top, twice, and it chirped twice.

"Yes, Captain, moving into position now," Watson replied over the COM.

"Place *the Roosevelt* in a tractor beam, Commander, and arrest the senior staff. We'll be bringing the rest up soon for the brig," Admiral Wainwright ordered.

"And have a shuttle bring Professor Ranko down to *the Gamma II* station," Jessica Wainwright ordered, looking at Bowers, and closed the link.

The plateau rocked again, forcing all that was standing to the ground, "Quake!" Jessica Macpherson called out. Mishophar's scream echoed in all directions.

"What the Hell?" Admiral Wainwright yelled as the ground shook again.

"Mishophar," Macpherson screamed.

"Explain yourself, boy!" Admiral Wainwright demanded, and Bowers vanished.

"Dan!" Jessica Wainwright yelled, not wishing to lose him again.

CHAPTER TWELVE

REBIRTH

BOWERS FOUND HIMSELF BACK in the central chamber, the larger one this time, he found on the screen thirteen years ago, with no writings on the walls, the ceiling now closed and the floor slowly lowering and getting darker. It stopped, and he could feel the room was larger. Six stone pits ignited around the room, and he could now tell the room was four times the size of the chamber above.

The walls are not stone, but metal, he thought as he ran his hand over the wall behind him. *Smooth to the touch, cool, and metallic. Is this a stone Pyramid or a starship?*

Mishophar rose slowly out of the floor sitting in his Throne, near the center of the room with his cowl down and his eyes glaring. Bowers turned and saw the Throne, and Mishophar, and heard his heavy breathing.

"Should have that looked at. . ." he said snickering.

Mishophar lunged at him. Bowers raised his hands and stopped him in midflight, and then dropped him, letting out a loud shriek as if a wounded animal cried out; he stood, roared again, and then leaped at Bowers.

Bowers shifted to his right as Mishophar slammed into the wall behind him. Bowers ducked behind the Throne. Mishophar unleashed red and white bolts from his fingertips, blasting the top of the Throne, it exploded, "Face me, you coward!" Mishophar yelled.

"We can talk about this, don't you think?" Bowers said as he came around the Throne slowly.

Mishophar blasted again, and the sparks tossed Bowers back and across the room, slamming him into the wall, then he slid down onto the floor.

"I'll take that as a no," Bowers said standing and raising his hands slowly as white sparks arced and crackled near his fingertips and built more, arcs from white to blue. He pulled back and pushed forward, blasting out across the room at Mishophar, it exploded around him, slamming him back into the wall, hard, and deep into the wall, and dropped back to the floor.

Mishophar just shook it off and stood, building arcs of his own. Bowers started running at him, building arcs, again too, sparks flying, and he lunged across the room, and they collided and exploded into a bright white light. The Throne shattered completely.

Bowers slowly awoke and was now face down, as the Sun shined through from above, the arrows were scattered all around, and the Throne was in rubble and scattered across the room. Mishophar's cloak laid on his back. He stood up and looked around, only seeing the debris and the six fire pits, then from behind him a white light slowly emerged through the bright Sun's rays. Illuminating the chamber more.

"You have done well, Daniel Bowers, with your first task," an Angelic voice stated through the light. He turned fast and a woman stood there in a white robe and a heavenly glow, floating a few meters above him, with golden-blonde hair.

"Task, and where is Mishophar?" Bowers asked.

"You were able to use the resonance and your new powers to destroy Mishophar."

"My powers?" Bowers demanded.

"You are the promised one, spoken of many millennia ago, who would come home, protect, and destroy the Ancient one."

"That was too easy."

"Yes, but you had the strength because you were the new, he was the old."

"I have no idea what you are talking about. Who are you!"

"You will know soon, *your* journey is just beginning," She said as she rose back up into the bright sunlight and disappeared.

The capstone of the Pyramid exploded, and all took cover.

"What the. . ." Admiral Wainwright yelled.

Caleb pointed toward the entrance, and they all saw Bowers exiting, Jessica Wainwright could tell he had more confidence than in the past, and they ran back to join him, "It's over, he's dead," Bowers explained.

"What, who?" Admiral Wainwright asked.

"Mishophar is dead, and I can finish my original mission," Bowers answered.

"As I recall, your original mission parameters, thirteen years ago—were to learn why the Pyramid was here, which you have. Why the planet was dead, and the carbon dioxide atmosphere, which is in two days?" Admiral Wainwright said.

"Yes, and I believe Professor Ranko can help us answer the carbon dioxide issue once we're all back at *Gamma II*. And if it was good for habitation? I feel now that Mishophar is gone the planet can restart itself, a rebirth," Bowers explained.

Jessica Wainwright smiled, took his hand, and he saw the ring on her finger that he was going to give her, and he smiled back.

"Well, good luck with all that, Commander, I am taking her and the others back to the other station and then Mars for questioning," Admiral Wainwright said, waved at Major George, and they left.

"So how do we get back to *my* team?" Macpherson asked looking from Bowers to Caleb.

Caleb pointed off to an area to their right at the cliff wall nearby. Caleb reached into the cliff wall, and into a small slit, and pulled down. A portion of the wall slid back into the cliff and turned, and a long tunnel emerged to a dead end. Caleb motioned for them to enter the small opening carved out of the tunnel near the back.

Bowers stepped in the small alcove last, and it dropped fast. All but Caleb hugged the walls.

The shaft stopped and as they stepped off, looked out over Eden, with rubble everywhere, and saw people cleaning up from the blasts. Caleb leads them down a set of stone stairs and back up to the great hall.

Mij'ha ran up to her Father and hugged him, "Is the shaking over?"

"Yes, love. Gon, this is Bowers, he destroyed the Ancient one." Caleb explained, Gon and all the people knelt around him, there were about fifty of them in the great hall.

"No, no, please stand," Bowers said, helping the old man to his feet.

Macpherson looked around for her people, "and where are my people?" Macpherson asked, now seeing his short leather pants and moccasins.

"They are good, some assistance needed, but good. Should not have used the platform, Caleb, during the blasts, not good," Gon said, as he motioned them back toward the large doors and down the block to a small brick building.

"Captain!" Calvin yelled, Macpherson was happy to see her whole team, and glad she lost no more crew members. The Swansons were lying on two beds, back against the far wall, Calvin and Hitchcock were standing as if they were disusing something when they entered. There were two Eden men at the doors they entered, in black robes, and cowls down.

Macpherson looked back at the doors, "Guards?" and pointed.

"No, no, Captain, just for our protection while they cleaned up, out there, said it was for our safety," Hitchcock explained, as Remy moved to each of the Swansons, pulled a screen from his white jacket, and ran it over each, one at a time.

"Both are good, just unconscious, Theresa has a broken leg," Remy explained and pointed back to Walker-Swanson. Walker-Swanson moaned, waking. "Easy, Kathy," Remy answered.

"Theresa, where's Theresa?" Walker-Swanson yelled, as she sat up quickly and looked around, then saw her across the room, and ran fast, "She's okay, Doc, right?"

Remy nodded. She laid down next to her wife, and Bowers turned back toward Gon and Caleb, "Now, *we* need to talk."

Gon led them out and into a large panoramic room with many screens, up on the angled high ceilings and walls that encircled the room, showing different points of the planet above, and a few men and women were working around the consoles, "This is how we watch the surface, to know when it is safe to go up. There, the day you returned," Gon said and pointed at one of the screens, which was showing the Pyramid.

A young woman in her twenties tapped at one of the consoles, and the screen changed tonight, and they could see Bowers as he was limping through the desert on his first night, bruised, lost, and confused.

Jessica Wainwright gasped and put her hand on Bowers's shoulder, then took his hand, "My god."

"Don't worry, *Gamma* was able to fix me up," Bowers said with a slight smile.

"*Gamma?*" Jessica Wainwright asked.

"The computer!" Hitchcock and Macpherson answered together.

"We see all here, and when we saw you there, and what the Prophetess had told us, we knew the new age was upon us," Gon explained.

Thunder cracked on a few screens, "Thunder? We've never heard any since we arrived. Lighting, and high winds, yes with storms but no thunder," Macpherson said. More thunder and clouds started forming, heavy and fast, and then rain. Water also rushed up on the surface from deep underground.

"Yes, Mishophar was holding back the true form of this planet, even whilst he slept, several years ago, the planet changed to the way it was now, but since you stopped him, the planet will now restore itself," Gon explained.

Bowers snapped his fingers. Macpherson's team, the Swansons, still on the bed, and the Doctor next to them, Gon, Caleb, and Jessica Wainwright appear on the surface with Bowers, back at the Pyramid with the other vehicles. The rain increased, more lightning, and thunder. Swanson awoke from the rain washing over her face. They all start celebrating, laughing, and feeling the rain wash over them. Most have never seen or felt rain before, with the closed systems on Earth and Mars.

Jessica Wainwright looked at Bowers deeply, smiling, and they kiss, "Damn, I've missed you, Dan."

He looked down at the ring, pulled her hand up to her face, the one he was going to give her, thinking they must have given her all his personal effects, and was happy.

Bowers snapped his fingers again, and this time they were back at *Gamma II*, in the conference room, all but Swanson and the Doctor, who returned to the medical bay, the table still up against the wall, and the remaining jeep and larger vehicles near the station outside.

Professor Ranko was working on some papers, he jumped as they appeared, the wall still down, and the room filling with water.

"How and where's Theresa?" Walker-Swanson screamed.

"He is the chosen one," Gon said.

"Good to have you all back, Captain. Ensign Swanson and Doctor Mabuto are in the medical bay, Lieutenant." *Gamma* replied.

"Your Uplink working, and your files restored?" Mitchell asked as he pushed on a section of the wall. The ledge and window rose back into place, stopping the water from flooding.

"Yes, once *the Roosevelt* was no longer jamming this sector, my Uplink was restored, and I was able to download new files and reboot my system," *Gamma* explained, "and where is Chief Adams? My sensors do not detect him on the planet."

"Dead, log it, please," Macpherson ordered.

Bowers crossed to Gon and Caleb, "We need to finish our talk," but turned slowly toward Ranko, "But first, Lucy, you got some splainin'," Bowers sarcastically said.

"Yes, we learned of the plan your Admiral Martinez wished for this planet; I do hope we have stopped him," Gon answered.

"Yes, but I mean the planets. Will you allow *us* to stay? It is *your* world?" Bowers asked.

Gon slapped Bowers on his shoulder, "Yes, our long-lost tribe has come home----yes, you are welcome. Our planet is *your* planet."

"Good to know, and how long will this rain continue?" Walker-Swanson asked, looking out the window, "And what's with your snapping power, Sir?" she said for the first time, with a sign of respect for him and his rank.

"As long as the planet needs to restart *her* rebirth. As it did many Danga cycles ago. Mishophar and his people were not of this world. They came here, enslaved us, took our resources, and when they bred with us, some of their descendants gained their powers. Very few have them today. He has the markers from the first ones, which is how he has the power. Mishophar allowed it to flourish that first day, when he attacked," Gon explained.

"Captain, a ship is entering orbit; it is *the Sun Tzu,* the President's ship, and it is firing upon *the Roanoke,* disabling her and *the Roosevelt,*" *Gamma* reported as the ground shook and Bowers vanished. Macpherson, Jessica Wainwright, and Walker-Swanson ran out.

Bowers appeared back in the Ancient ship, tapped on the table a few times, and the ship rose into space, in line with *the Sun Tzu,* both ships facing off; the shield of the Ancient ship absorbing *the Sun Tzu's* beams. Firing again but still no damage, and in a flash, faster than any of the current quantum point-to-point drives, it was gone.

Bowers was shocked as he watched out the large window, as the *Sun Tzu* vanished, and knowing the ship had technology from *the Andromeda Galaxy.*

He opened the COM, "*Roanoke,* how is the ship?"

"Down, but not out, Engineer Hoffman and Commander Watson are working on it, thanks for the assist, Commander?" Admiral Wainwright answered back, "How did they leave so fast?"

"It has technology from *the Andromeda Galaxy,* never reported."

"Damn him!" Admiral Wainwright said with disgust, "And I see it is now raining down there."

"The dead world Professor Ranko told us about was only dead because of Mishophar. He is now dead, and the planet is in the process of a rebirth."

"I await your report, Commander," Admiral Wainwright answered.

Bowers watched the rainstorm from above the planet. Washing over the world, and streams starting again, filling deep canyons with oceans, the beauty of this blue-green jewel was starting again, and it was beautiful, Earth and Mars had a chance, and he knew Humanity had a chance, too, as he lowered the Ancient ship back near the Pyramid.

Bowers appeared back in the conference room, shocking Ranko again, "Professor, I thought we were friends."

"We are?" Ranko said standing up again.

"Then why did you lie about the carbon dioxide period of this planet, and tell everyone that it took place in forty-eight hours?"

"I was under duress, Admiral Martinez told me if I did not cooperate, I would disappear, and we both know he could accomplish that," Ranko explained.

"So, he created a lie?" Bowers asked.

"Yes, I then documented it, and the President and Cooper kept repeating the story till everyone believed it, including Admiral Nagoya. You repeat a lie long enough, it can become the truth."

"Thank you, old friend," Bowers said, knowing how gullible people can be.

"Report, *Gamma!*" Macpherson ordered, entering Command.

"I am registering Commander Bowers back on the Ancient ship and raising the ship over the planet, between *the Sun Tzu,* and *the Roanoke. The Sun Tzu* fired twice, but my sensor reported the Ancient ship absorbed the blasts, and then *the Sun Tzu* vanished faster than my sensors could report." *Gamma* answered.

"And Dan?" Jessica Wainwright asked.

"Here, my love," Bowers answered from behind her. They all turned back, as Gon and Caleb joined them, and Hitchcock stood outside the door for them to enter.

"All the commotion over?" Caleb asked.

"Yes, I think it will be sometime before the President returns. He'll nurse his wounds. *Gamma,* please contact Admiral Wainwright on *the Roanoke?*" Bowers asked.

"Wainwright here," Admiral Wainwright appeared on the vid screen.

"Sir, I believe, knowing Martinez, and his conspirators, brought you here. Who all did you find, other than Martinez and the President involved?"

"Senator Cooper, Martinez, and the President were all that Admiral Fitzsimmons, Senator Macomb, and I could learn of as the ring leaders."

"I think, they just left for *the Andromeda* Galaxy. I learned when I first came here, after meeting with Martinez and Admiral Nagoya; he wanted this for a staging point."

"Yes, hopefully, we've stopped him," Admiral Wainwright said as the screen split, "have you been listening, Madam Vice President?" Vice President Appleton and Senator Macomb appear on the new screen.

Bowers saw his old technician, "Good to see you, Apple—Madam Vice President."

"Yes, ten years ago, before I came into office, the then President ordered Admiral Martinez and *the Roosevelt* to go into *the Andromeda Galaxy* and learn what they could, he never documented a thing." Vice President Appleton explained.

"Yes, we will need to investigate that, no to," Senator Macomb said standing behind Vice President Appleton and she nodded in agreement, Bowers knew then this was his next assignment.

"Bowers, you, and Macpherson's team, once you finish up there, regroup with Captain Wainwright and *the Roanoke,* and look into that, please" Vice President Appleton ordered, as her side of the screen went black.

Macpherson turned and nodded to Jessica Wainwright, "We're with you, Dan," Jessica Wainwright said.

"Without Martinez, you think they both will continue with their plan for *Andromeda?*" Bowers asked Admiral Wainwright.

"There is a good chance. I learned from Admiral Fitzsimmons recently, and with the alien technology, Cooper and the President got off Mars, with a transporting device that was found in *Andromeda,* and with what I just saw with *the Sun Tzu,* anything is possible. This may not be *their* staging point, but it will be *ours.*" Admiral Wainwright answered.

Bowers slowly laid down in his quarters; it had been a long few weeks, wondering what Martinez was up to now with *Andromeda* and the future. Something told him Martinez was not dead and their wrestling match was far from over, they both had eluded Thanatos, the messenger of death, many times before. He awoke back in the central chamber, looking up at the bright heavenly angel again, thinking it was just a dream.

"This is not a dream, Daniel Bowers," she said.

"Why am I back here?"

"You are right, he is still alive, and you need to stop him, or the Galaxies will not survive."

"Who are you?" he yelled, only to wake up back in his quarters, lightning flashed than thunder. He looked out the window, seeing all the vegetation growing fast, and pondering what all had happened, what Martinez had planned for him, next time. And his new powers…

ABOUT THE AUTHOR

Joshua Quentin Hawk, Thomas Roy Bass, hails from Portsmouth, Virginia, has lived in Texas and California, now presently in San Diego, California. After many years of medical issues, due to kidney failure and transplant, and then failure again, he now has the time to write. He has worked in the Tech Industry in the past as a Network Engineer and has studied Geological, Environmental, and Oceanographic Sciences, as well as Psychology, Criminology, and Forensic Psychology.

He has always wanted to be a writer, so he told himself, "I have the time." Hawk has wished to be a published author since he was in high school.

This is Hawk's first published book.